A Place And A Name

by

Phil Hadley

To Ken & Alison
I trust you enjoy this
second dose of wartime
Cornwall.
God bless,
Phil

ISBN 978 1 9998463 1 2

Published 2020
Phil Hadley Publishing
Cornwall

Printed on recycled paper.

Printed by
R Booth Ltd, Penryn, Cornwall

Dedicated to

my very awesome son

&

in memory of

the crew of HMS Registan,
especially those who lost their lives on 27th May 1941
and those whose grave is the waters off
the Cornish coast,

&

The 'Silent Keys' of the Radio Security Service

"At the going down of the sun, and in the morning,
we will remember them."

ACKNOWLEDGEMENTS

I acknowledge the role my late parents and sister played in creating and nurturing my interest in things historical and that of my History Teacher, Mike England, who helped to develop that academically. Thanks to my family and friends who have encouraged this second journey into historical fiction.

Thank you to Andrew Newson who provides a great service allowing me to access files in the National Archives from the comfort of my own home.

Thanks to the ever helpful Peter & Sqeez & team at Booths for all your assistance and professionalism in difficult times.

Thanks to all those members of the wartime generation who over many years have shared their experiences and snippets of information that help bring this story alive & give it authenticity. We owe you so much for your service and sacrifice.

Thanks to the veterans of the Radio Security Service for sharing their stories and expertise and allowing me to attend one of their reunions at Bletchley Park. Special thanks to Don Wallis who shared his memories of St Erth and to the sons of the late Harry Griffiths who allowed me access to his wartime diary and notebook. Thanks too to Stan Ames, the RSS archivist, for sharing much information and expertise.

Thanks to the relatives of the survivors and casualties of HMS Registan who have shared their thoughts, memories and stories with me.

Finally, thanks to you the reader, and I know you will join with me in saying:

"At the going down of the sun and in the morning
we will remember them."

Laurence Binyon "For The Fallen", The Times, September 1914

"A nation that forgets its past
has no future."

Sir Winston Churchill 1874-1965

PROLOGUE

The silhouette of the plane glided across the waves in the moonlight. The sea was a shimmering mirror where the streaks of moonlight cast their long fingers through the breaks in the cloud. To either side it seemed a dark quivering mass that rose and fell like the chest of a giant beast.

Johann sat mesmerised from his vantage point behind the pilots. It was nine months since his last mission in England. Going back filled him with a heady mix of excitement and apprehension. The Junkers 52 had left Chartres with the taskforce of Heinkel III's who were to target an airfield on the north coast of Cornwall. Johann glanced left and right and admired the pilots who had kept the three planes either side in strict formation all the way across the Channel. More followed behind but he could not see them from where he was perched.

One of the pilots broke the silence. "Dodman three miles ahead." His fellow pilot acknowledged and then turned to Johann. "That's the enemy coast ahead. You'd better go and get yourself ready." Johann rose and stole a look towards the Cornish cliffs and then turned and waddled into the body of the plane. The dispatcher stood up and helped him towards the door. Johann then stood arms out while the dispatcher checked the straps for the umpteenth time, hitched up the static line, adjusted his helmet and then shouted in his ear, "You're all good to go!"

Johann swallowed. This would be his first parachute jump in a combat situation. He had done a number while at the Stendal Parachute Training School completing six successfully to get his Parachutist's Badge. It was a mark of the importance of his mission, and of the regard his superiors held him in, that he had been given such extensive training. He had heard of some agents being sent into England without jump training. The thought made him shudder as he pictured an agent called Josef who, having had no parachute training, was reported to have been captured after he broke his ankle on landing back in January.

Suddenly the aircraft shook as an explosion rocked the air. They had crossed the coast and the anti-aircraft gun at Hemmick had opened up on the formation coming in low. Fortunately the shells were exploding above them, the gunners not yet having found their range. But their arrival was now being announced to all and sundry. The pilots noted the position of the gun – that would have to be dealt with on another occasion, especially as the headland was such a useful navigational tool. The engines strained as the aircraft was climbing. Johann rested his hands above the door gazing down through the small window. He couldn't see much. A searchlight had come on off to the west and its finger of light was roaming the sky but it wasn't aimed in their direction.

They levelled out at the drop height. The dispatcher put his hand to his ear as he strained to hear the message on the intercom. He held up three fingers. Three minutes to the drop zone. Johann gave him a nod. He felt his heart beginning to race. He tried to make out features on the ground below but it was just one dark mass.

The aircraft banked as they turned indicating they were now leaving the stream of bombers. This was the second night in a row the Heinkels had left France for the Cornish airfields. Last night St Eval, Trebelsue and Portreath had all been hit. Tonight St Eval was the only target to act as cover for his insertion into Cornwall. He had sat in on the briefing given to the pilots as they were told to hit not only the airfield but the dispersed sites in the countryside round about. The bomb loads were far heavier than the night before. Johann was glad. 'It might keep the enemy's heads down,' he thought.

His ruminations were interrupted as the dispatcher stepped up, ushered him back and opened the door. The cold night air whistled into the fuselage. The dispatcher, stood just to the side of the door, held up one finger. Johann waddled back into position and the dispatcher rested one hand on his back while the other clasped a handle on the stanchion next to the door. 'He's going to push me out if I don't jump,' Johann thought to himself. In fact, it was the only way to communicate when to go to the parachutist as Johann couldn't see from his position the green light that would be flicked on by the pilot as they reached the drop zone. He was just thinking it's taking a long time coming when he felt a hefty shove in the back and in an instant he had stepped forward and was dropping into the darkness.

The rush of cold air snatched his breath away. The wind whistled in his ears. Faster and faster he was falling until the static line pulled his parachute open from the pack on his back. The silk bundle slowly unravelled and then suddenly billowed and opened fully and his rapid decent was slowed. Johann gasped for air and took several deep breaths. He glanced up with relief acknowledging every parachutist's prayer that their canopy will open. As his swaying lessened he now looked down keen to make out the landmarks that would guide him into the chosen landing ground. The wind was taking him north east and he knew if he went too far that way he would fall into a steeply sided wooded valley. Suddenly he began to make out the hedgerows that divided the patchwork of fields. He had just decided to aim for the largest when the sound of explosions in the distance made the hairs on the back of his neck stand up. He glanced round towards the coast and realised the bombing of St Eval had begun. Tracer shots could be seen going skywards as the defences opened up on the incoming bomber stream. He could not watch for too long because the ground was now rising to meet him at an alarming speed and he readied himself for landing, tugging on his chords to adjust the canopy as best he could.

With a thud he was down and rolling and then came to a sudden stop sprawled on his back. He was winded and lay there for a few seconds, before the training kicked in and he scrambled to his knees and began pulling in his parachute. Speed was of the essence if he was to get away undetected from this spot. Folding the billowing silk to squeeze the air out and make it as small as he could he began looking around for the best place to conceal it. After a minute or two of hauling in the uncooperative canopy he had it in a bundle where he could pick it up and move to the edge of the field. Again he was grateful that he had landed albeit roughly, but mercifully uninjured. Looking around for a suitable spot to bury his parachute, he slid the small rucksack off his back and began to fumble for the small shovel. He pulled both the spade and the handle shaft out and was just about to slot them together when he noticed a gap in the Cornish stone wall behind him. Instantly an idea formed in his mind and within a couple of minutes he had removed several of the stones, dug out the earth behind to create a chamber for the parachute, squashed it in and began to replace the stones to hide it. He glanced around but there was no sign of anyone approaching. In the distance were the muffled explosions of the raid on St Eval. "It was certainly getting a pasting tonight," he thought thankful that the Luftwaffe crews had been true to their promise that they would create such a scene of devastation that no one would notice his silent arrival. He started to kick away the earth he couldn't replace but then stopped. How foolish to get his shoes caked in mud, so he bent down with the shovel and began to spread it out as best he could. "A heavy shower before dawn would be most helpful," he thought, "but not until I'm well on my way from here." Deciding he could linger no longer just in case his descent had been spotted, he took the shovel apart and replaced it in his rucksack, slung the bag over one shoulder and headed along the hedge until he could find an exit.

He clambered over the five bar gate and stepped into the lane. "Right or left?" he pondered. "Right is going downhill so will take me to the river Fal. I want to go west, so it must be left."

He walked at a brisk pace. He wanted to run but thought it would be more suspicious if he was spotted. He kept going. He didn't know it but those that lived in those parts called it 'Carnwinnick Lane'. Soon he was at the top of the hill. He looked back. Silence. Save for the distant crepitations of the bombs at St Eval. He turned and continued on his way.

Chapter One

Elizabeth stood beside the sleek shape of the black Humber Snipe as she waited for the liaison officer to emerge from the hut where he had been meeting his RAF counterpart in the Station Headquarters at RAF St Eval. The powerful car was her pride and joy. It had been ever since she had been chosen to drive it last summer for the Major. What a summer that had been! Her ATS superiors were impressed by the report they received indicating Driver Treluckey had been very helpful in the locating of an enemy agent whilst acting as the Major's chauffeur, had remained calm under fire and demonstrated both a good knowledge of Cornwall's winding roads and a superb handling of the car. She had beamed with pride when a few weeks later she was awarded her first stripe moving from the rank of Volunteer to Chief Volunteer. How the other girls in the dorm had teased her. They were aware of how she had fallen head over heels in love with the handsome Major who had spent a week in Cornwall, managed to get himself shot and then after one mysterious night that Elizabeth was reluctant to talk about had swanned back off to London. After a weekend appearance shortly afterwards it seemed the only contact was a weekly letter that arrived for CV Treluckey but she remained tight-lipped about her dalliance with this mysterious man.

Now on her shoulder was a second stripe as further promotion had come her way in the spring. Sub-Leader Treluckey had made her parents proud when she broke the news, although only last Friday she had been summoned into Section Leader Buscombe's office to be told she was now to be known as a Corporal. Apparently the War Office were reorganising the ranks as a step towards the full militarisation of the Service and their rank structure would now fall in line with the rest of the Army. Just a change in name, no change in the number of stripes.

"That should stop some of the jeers from the men around the barracks," she had thought as she stepped out of the office. "They'll now have some idea of the rank I hold." Some hope it had been. "They must be getting desperate if they're making lasses corporals," one friendly Scots soldier had ribbed her. Elizabeth had got her own back by making him salute her superior rank which caused him to be the subject of much merriment amongst his pals.

She stroked her stripes with her gloved hand, then rubbed the wing of the car as she noticed some finger marks show up on the polished bodywork in the moonlight that had broken through the cloud. That was when she jumped. The deafening wail of the air raid siren had begun near the Watch Hut and was then sounded at several different locations across the airfield. The rise and fall of the haunting note of the sirens was a sound that filled Elizabeth with dread. She looked around in the darkness wondering where she should go for shelter, when the hut door behind her burst open and out came her officer and several RAF chaps.

"Come with us, Corporal" shouted Liaison Officer Batten as he followed the RAF officers across the tarmac apron towards the flagstaff. Elizabeth didn't need telling twice. It wasn't quite a run. All the training and advice was to "Do not rush. Take cover quietly," so it would encourage others to do the same. However, this little party was moving faster than a walk or a march. St Eval had been hit scores of times in enemy air raids that its personnel weren't for lingering.

Elizabeth was now aware of people moving in all sorts of directions. She glanced around. Many were going to man their posts and she felt a tinge of guilt that she was heading for the shelter.

"Come on, miss!" encouraged a friendly female voice from behind her. "Don't stand there gawping." She turned to see two WAAFs who had come from the guard room were also headed across the tarmac in the direction of the shelter.

Slowly they filed down the slope, into the brick entrance, past the blast wall and into the gloom of the shelter. Constructed of concrete sections that had been bolted together, the shelter rose to a height of about seven feet in the centre with the roof curving down to the ground on either side. Along each side were wooden benches and the assembled group were taking their seats. Elizabeth sat down next to the two WAAFs. Batten was with the RAF chaps on the opposite side.

"Usually about this time," said one of the RAF officers looking at his watch in the dim light from the two electric bulbs mounted in the ceiling giving a faint blue light glow.

"Nah! He's two minutes early," said another trying to inject some humour into the sombre looking assembly.

Elizabeth turned to the WAAFs at her side. She couldn't help feeling their azure uniforms looked smarter than hers. Not wanting to sound scared, Elizabeth asked hesitantly, "Does the airfield get raided often?"

"Almost every night since the beginning of the year, isn't it?" replied the one nearer to her with quite a head of auburn hair. She looked a little younger than Elizabeth and spoke with a Welsh accent.

"That's why they've moved our quarters down to Watergate Bay. So we're only here when we are on duty," added the other girl. She had a rounded face with a button nose and locks of wavy hair that poked out from underneath her cap. Elizabeth couldn't quite place her accent but thought it originated from somewhere along the south English coast.

"I don't mind. We're nearer the beach. Not that we can go swimming there because of the mines and the barbed wire. Have to go into Towan Beach in Newquay if we want a swim," she added.

"You've only been once! Said the water was too cold," the Welsh girl interjected.

"That's once more than you!" her colleague shot back.

"There's more interesting things to see when I go to Newquay," the Welsh lass said with a grin.

"Things! You mean men," said the other sarcastically.

"Aw, don't. Maybe I do. Better than swimming, anyway." Elizabeth could see these two were obviously good friends as well as sharing their duties, or perhaps, because of sharing their duties. The teasing was given with no offence being taken by the other. It reminded her of the girls back at Barracks in Bodmin. From a diverse group of strangers they had moulded into a well organised, well-disciplined company. There were the odd one or two that didn't seem to fit or take to the duties but they didn't stay long. It's probably the same for the Air Force girls surmised Elizabeth.

In the lull in the conversation, the girls became aware of another sound. All eyes looked towards the roof, not that you could see through it, but the noise that was heard came from above. The familiar sound of the drone of aircraft engines.

"Heinkels," said one of the RAF chaps.

"The heavies," added another. "Means we are in for a pasting tonight."

"Might be St Merryn's turn," said a third, more in hope than conviction. "Like the time Lord Haw-Haw boasted St Eval would be erased from the map and then had to apologise the next night when they had hit the wrong airfield!"

"You shouldn't be listening to him," said an RAF officer seated somewhere down the shelter in the gloom.

"Does the airfield get hit often?" asked Elizabeth of her two new companions. "I mean, do the bombs cause much damage?" she added preferring to talk of damage rather than casualties.

"About eighty bombs last night, they reckon," replied the Welsh WAAF.

“Damaged one of the hangers and a few of the aircraft,” the other added.

“Was anyone….?” Elizabeth’s voice tailed off as she thought the worst.

“Only one civilian casualty. Just injured, not killed. Quite remarkable really,” continued the English girl.

“Unlike back in January when they scored a direct hit on one of the shelters by the Watch Tower. Hit right on the entrance.” It was a Welsh accent that was tinged with horror as it spoke. “Killed twenty one outright and another died from his injuries the following day. Poor blighters – didn’t stand a chance.”

“We won’t have any of that defeatist talk in here please, ACW Thomas,” came the clipped tones of an RAF officer out of the darkness.

“No, sir. Sorry, sir,” she replied sheepishly. The silent pause that followed found Elizabeth staring in horror at the prospect of dying in a concrete tomb. She shivered but it was not through cold. “At least the Lord was merciful in that it was quick,” she thought, hoping the injured man hadn’t suffered too much before succumbing to his wounds.

“Please Lord, may I make it out of here alright tonight,” she prayed silently.

The silence was shattered by a huge explosion, followed by another a few seconds later. In all there were six, each one sounding closer than the last, as the stick of bombs fell in a line across the Cornish countryside.

“Sounds like they were over the road,” said one of the RAF officers obviously trying to pinpoint where the bombs had landed and so calculate any damage that was likely to have occurred.

In the half an hour that followed Elizabeth lost track of all the explosions. Some were close and some were further away. They were mixed in with the noise of the anti-aircraft guns responding: Bofors and machine guns adding to the cacophony of sound that battered her eardrums even through the concrete of the shelter. Conversation was impossible and the shelter’s occupants were left alone with their thoughts and their prayers.

Several times when the explosions were so close the ground shook, Elizabeth was left picturing her parents, Francis and Hannah Treluckey, and her younger brother, David, at home on their farm overlooking the Camel estuary. She wished she was there now. Then she remembered that the farm was only four and a half miles from where she was sat so the raid would be impacting them as well. She knew her father, if he were not on duty with the Home Guard, would have ushered her mother and brother as soon as the sirens had sounded into the Anderson shelter he had dug into the farmhouse garden. This shelter was certainly stronger than that, so she prayed that they would be preserved. Then she could see in her mind’s eye, her beloved Zac as he leaned out of the carriage window and kissed her for the last time before the train had left the station and returned Major Isaac Trevennel to London. That was last summer. She had worried about him as she had read the newspaper accounts of the Blitz upon London but his weekly letters reassured her that he was safe and well. Only once when he had described the fires around St Paul's Cathedral just after Christmas did she get a sense of him being in any danger. Some week's he had said he was travelling with work and so was out of harm's way but never gave any indication of where he might be. Then she worried whether anywhere in Britain was safe. Many of the troops at the barracks had thought they were coming to a quiet spot in being posted to Cornwall only to have a rude awakening. Many of the evacuees, when their parents realised just how many air raids Cornwall was having, took their children home again. She just hoped Zac wasn't worrying about her! How she longed to feel his strong arms around her again. There was something about the touch of a loved one that assured you all was okay with the world and fortified you for whatever life may throw at you.

The explosion was deafening. Dust fell from the roof and several of the shelter's occupants coughed. No one screamed. Just the controlled tones of the RAF officer's voice.

"That were close," he said in an expression revealing his Black Country roots that his earlier clipped tone had belied. For a while no one spoke. They all knew that last bomb had been very close. Then the firing stopped. The anti-aircraft guns had fallen silent. Two minutes later the all clear sounded. Everyone stood up, brushing dust off their uniforms in the dim light. Slowly they edged towards the exit and duly filed out into the night.

Elizabeth breathed deeply taking in the night air. There was an acrid smell and Elizabeth could taste the dust on her tongue. The RAF chaps were suddenly all talking and calling as they became aware of airmen rushing off to her right. She could make out the silhouette of the operations block but everyone seemed to be heading beyond that. She looked around for Batten and saw he was talking to the RAF officer. She stood waiting for direction when a young airman came up to the officer, saluted and obviously passed on some message. She was just too far away to be able to hear. As the young airman left, Batten shook hands with the officer and turned towards Elizabeth.

"We can find the car now. My business here is done and if we stay we'll only be in the way," he said as he approached. "That's assuming the car's unscathed. They seem to have caught a packet tonight. Apparently both the officers' mess and the sergeants' mess have been virtually demolished."

"Anyone…?" Elizabeth didn't need to ask any more.

"They fear fatalities but until they can account for everyone they won't know," he replied as they turned towards the roadway in front of the station headquarters where they had left the car.

It was still there. It had a thin covering of dust and a few splinters of wood on it. She guessed one of the wooden huts had been blown to smithereens. Elizabeth walked round the vehicle looking for any signs of damage but there didn't appear to be any, although she thought that daylight might reveal some markings on the paintwork. She held open the door and Batten got in. Elizabeth went round to the driver's door, got in, inserted the key and started the ignition. To her relief the engine purred into life. She turned on the lights and gently edged forward. It would be a slow drive home as the Lucas Maxlite headlight covers would not allow more than the regulation amount of light to show and that would make negotiating the twisting Cornish roads back to Bodmin a challenge.

As she approached the gate she slowed while the guard stepped out of the hut and lifted the barrier. As she pulled away Elizabeth couldn't help wondering where the two airmen on guard duty had sheltered during the air raid and concluded they had probably stayed at their post all through. She turned left into the road and headed for St Columb. She would be glad when her head hit the pillow back in barracks tonight. It had been quite an evening. At least she would have a tale to tell Zac in her next letter though she'd have to be careful how she worded it in order to get it past the censor. But that would have to wait for another day. She needed all her concentration now to get both her passenger and herself safely back.

Chapter Two

Mr Owen's office was unpretentious. He sat behind a large mahogany desk with an ornate desk lamp on one corner and a telephone on the other. On the solitary shelf on the wall stood a row of large leather bound ledgers that dated back to 1910. There were three hard back chairs dotted about the room with a filing cabinet in one corner near the window. The window was divided into three, each having eight panes of glass and looked down into the yard where the Major had left his Humber Snipe. This was the Central Office of the Cornwall Electric Power Company which had made great strides in providing a lot of Cornwall with its electricity over the last twenty years. This site, originally the power station for the Camborne-Redruth tramway, had grown into the main office, as well as being a sub-station for providing electricity to the local mines and engineering works.

Mr Owen paused before he spoke, choosing his words carefully.

"So let me get this right. You want to run an exercise that will test our security at the Hayle Power Station."

"That is correct," replied the Major.

"While our employees do their bit within the plant, you realise that the perimeter of the site is in the hands of the army, currently a regiment from Yorkshire."

"I do, which is why I've asked you to set up a meeting of your Hayle superintendent and the officer in charge for two o'clock this afternoon."

"So you are going to warn them about the exercise?" asked the company chairman, a little perplexed at this dramatic scenario descending on his business.

"In the same way the nation has been warned about the possibility of Hitler's invasion and we are called to be vigilant, I shall inform them that their defences and security are to be tested and they should be vigilant," explained the Major.

"It's a little inconvenient, but as you have shown me, you have the authority to carry out such an enterprise. I am confident, however, that our measures and those taken by the soldiers are sufficient that you will not be able to penetrate the power station to any extent so as to compromise its working."

"We shall see," said the Major with a glint in his eye that betrayed the fact he was relishing the challenge. What the Major could not divulge to this avuncular Cornishman was that following the success of Operation Claymore – the Commando raid on the Lofoten Islands off the coast of Norway in March – Churchill was worried about the Germans trying similar kinds of raids on British soil and so had ordered a review of security at numerous strategic installations that were crucial to the local infrastructure and consequently the war effort.

Major Isaac Trevennel, working for MI(R), Military Intelligence Research – a cover name for a small unit answerable only to Churchill that had overseen the formation of the Independent Companies used in Norway and the Auxiliary Units set up in Britain in the summer of 1940 to harry a German invasion – often told inquisitive officers that he worked for the Inter Service Research Bureau. When Churchill had briefed him on his latest responsibility the Major chose to return to his home county to test out the security of a number of key installations, some of which were classed as Category A – to be defended at all costs. So it was on this bright May morning he found himself in the company offices of the main electricity supplier in Cornwall, the only one with a power station connected since 1933 to the National Grid, arranging for a meeting with the Hayle Power Station superintendent.

Mr Owen picked up the phone on his desk.

"Operator, can you get me Hayle 3176 please? Yes, yes, my number is Camborne 2201. Yes, it's urgent. I'll hold until you have the connection. Thank you." He raised an eyebrow at the smartly dressed officer sat looking at him. The Major simply smiled back. Mr Owen was a confident businessman. He had only been in the top post a couple of years since his predecessor retired but he had overseen the company cope with all the vagaries of wartime demand. In the winter of 1939 into 1940 the company had its stations working at maximum capacity for only the second time in their history due to the prolonged cold, icy spell that had seen heavy falls of snow even in Cornwall. For Hayle, that had been working at a generating capacity of 27,800 kilowatts. There had also been numerous new military installations that had all required power, to say nothing of the new aerodromes that were now being constructed on the narrow peninsula that formed England's longest county. He was rightly proud that his company was meeting the challenges the war posed, but now the spectre of a security exercise raised its head he hoped it would pass as a minor inconvenience rather than escalate into a major headache.

"Connecting you now, sir," came the sweet voice of the operator. Mr Owen adjusted his grip on the handset and said,

"Peller, is that you? Ah, good, Fred. I have a little matter I need you to deal with. I have here a Major from the army, a Major Trevennel, and he's coming down to see you. Will you get hold of the officer in command of the soldiers guarding your plant and Major Trevennel will meet the two of you in your office at two o'clock this afternoon. Can't say any more than that at this stage. Oh and not a word to anyone. The Major will explain all when he sees you. Yes, two o'clock. Got it? Good man. Thank you."

The Major smiled at the effective and efficient way Mr Owen dealt with those under his authority as the businessman replaced the handset.

"Mr Peller will meet you at two o'clock. He can provide any further information you require on Hayle," said Mr Owen satisfied he had met the Major's request.

"Thank you for your co-operation. I am sure this exercise will be to everyone's benefit. Better to try out the security with friends than for the first time with the enemy." The Major stood as he spoke indicating the meeting was over. He held out his hand across the desk to Mr Owen. The businessman rose and shook it firmly.

"I'm sure Mr Peller will keep me informed on how things progress," he said.

"You'll get a full report from me debriefing you after the event before I report back to my superior in London," said the Major not wanting to divulge he was answerable directly to the Prime Minister. He turned on his heels, placed his cap and headed for the door. There was a spring in his step as he descended the stone stairway two steps at a time. Once outside the door he glanced back at the sign above it.

"Cornwall Electric Power Company. I think you are in for a shock!" he said to himself as he opened his car door. Usually the Major was entitled to a driver, but for this journey he had insisted on driving himself. The engine purred into life and he eased out of the yard and onto the main road.

A few minutes later he pulled up to park in Cross Street in Camborne and made his way into a small café just along from the Berriman's bus stop for Troon. It was here just over an hour before he had dropped his three passengers and as he entered the café he saw them sat at a table in the far corner. He joined them. Their empty plates showed they had enjoyed the meal and he asked whether they wanted a cup of tea.

When the waitress came to the table the Major ordered a pot of tea for four and a pasty for himself. Fortunately this Cornish staple had not suffered too much from the war, though it was fair to say it was now more vegetable than steak!

Once the waitress had disappeared all eyes were on the Major. He looked round the table at the keen faces and smiled.

"We're on for two o'clock this afternoon," he said. Instinctively the three checked their watches. Fifty five minutes to go.

"How long will it take us to get there, sir?" asked Ken. He was a young man, late twenties, an athletic frame, wavy hair and hazel eyes.

"It will be about twenty minutes in the car," the Major replied, "So you can enjoy your cup of tea."

"How do you propose getting us inside in broad daylight?" asked Daniel. He was the eldest of the three at thirty two but was probably the fittest. He was married which also set him apart from his companions. He had played football for the county before the war. He had a kindly face with a short beard.

"Two in the boot and one under the rug on the floor of the back seat," the Major said matter of factly. The three men stared in disbelief.

"There is a sizeable boot on the Humber Snipe and I've made sure it's empty," said the Major by way of explanation. "After my meeting just now, they will be so focused on me that they won't check the car. Just you wait and see."

"Permission to ask, sir, how on earth did you dream this idea up?" asked Matthew. He was the youngest of the group and always full of questions. He had a head of curly red hair, green eyes and a boyish grin.

“I saw it done in a silent short I saw at the picture house as a child. Could have been Keystone Cops or something of that ilk. I’ve forgotten the film but the ruse has stayed with me.” The three men stared at the Major in disbelief not knowing if he was giving an honest answer or pulling their legs. “I am sure we can pull it off,” the Major concluded leaving them to believe a silent comedy had been the inspiration for the operation they were now about to undertake.

“And what happens if we get caught?” asked Matthew. The Major paused before replying as the waitress brought in a tray with a pot of tea, four tea cups and a jug of milk. She placed it on the table and the Major instinctively picked up a spoon, lifted the lid on the pot and gave the tea a good stir.

“Then we go to Plan B,” he said.

“Which is?” said Ken and Daniel together.

“Put you in the coal wagons and send you down the wharf branch line when the Roskear train goes for its coal.”

“I think we’ll stick with Plan A,” said Matthew who could envisage them covered in coal dust leaving a trail wherever they went.

The Major’s pasty arrived and he picked it up and took a bite as the three men began to discuss who was going in the boot. The Major smiled. He knew he had done well when he chose to take men from the Fowey Auxiliary Unit. Its sergeant, Percy Robbins, had hand-picked the men. Daniel was the first choice as he had worked for several years in the Power House at Fowey and so had some knowledge of electrical installations.

Ken and Matthew had developed a reputation in the Unit for their stealth and so seemed eminently suitable for the operation. The Major sensed the men were at ease with each other and so should work well together to accomplish what he had in mind.

Having devoured his pasty and paid the bill, the Major led the three men to the car. Daniel sat in front alongside the Major with Ken and Matthew in the rear seat. As they turned into Church Street to head west on the A30, the Major began to give a little more detail on what was expected of the men.

"Your task is to place magnetic limpet mines on as much of the plant as you can access. The turbine and transformer are key. But I also want you to have a little but of fun. There's an extra pint for the chap who can place one in the control room, and the same for whoever can get down into the tunnel where all the high voltage cables leave the building to feed the rest of the county."

The men looked at each other and smiled. The Major sensed they were up for the challenge.

"Are these mines live?" asked Matthew.

"No, you've just got dummies but the real thing are now being used on some of the most secret operations our forces are undertaking and to devastating effect," replied the Major. The major pulled one out of the shelf in the dashboard and passed it to the men in the back. The Auxiliary Units were used to being well equipped but this was a new toy to the three men and they were delighted at the opportunity to use even just the dummy version. It would certainly give them kudos amongst the rest of the Unit. The two inch metal disc was about the size of a large hand span and surprisingly light in weight. Ken turned it over and saw the word "dummy" painted in red. He put it on the door of the car. It stayed in place.

"The magnets will hold it in place on any metal object," explained the Major who was equally impressed with Cecil Clarke's and Stuart Macrae's deadly little invention. "So in the power station you should find plenty of steel and be able to leave them where they won't be obvious at first glance."

"Albert would be so disappointed not to be in on this little job," said Daniel referring to their Unit's explosive expert. "He would love to get his hands on a set of these. He enjoys making things go bang!"

"So the plan is, I'll drive in and park in a quiet corner. When I'm inside seeing the station superintendent, you can slip out and find some cover. Then under the cover of darkness you can wreak your havoc."

"What happens if we get caught?" asked Ken.

"That's why you are in military uniform, so you'll have the rights of a POW and not be shot by the Nazis as a spy," replied the Major with a twinkle in his eye.

"Oh jolly," said Matthew with a touch of sarcasm.

"They could interrogate you and torture you. So it's a chance to show just of what the men of the Auxiliary Units are made."

"Are we allowed to use force, if necessary?" asked Matthew.

“No, it’s a security exercise, not a military exercise,” replied the Major. “The power station employees are all civilians and so must not be harmed. The soldiers who guard the perimeter are from the West Yorkshire Regiment and I’m hoping a bit of Cornish cunning and stealth will teach them a thing or two.”

“Don’t worry,” said Ken with a smile. “We won’t let them forget their stay in Cornwall.”

“Where are we going to lie low until it gets dark?” asked Daniel.

“Near where I am hoping to park the car there are some outbuildings and sheds. Hopefully you can duck into one of those without raising suspicions. Because their perimeter is patrolled constantly I fear the power station workers have got a little lax with their routines and from my observations yesterday have taken to leaving some of the sheds unlocked during daylight. You should have a choice of several depending on how many people are around.”

“So you’ve cased the joint already?” asked Ken with a grin.

“I spent a couple of hours observing from the church tower on the other side of the river. Most revealing,” said the Major, without explaining exactly what he had seen. “Whatever you do, don’t come outside the perimeter and go in the dunes. The beach has been mined!”

“Now he tells us. I wouldn’t have brought my bathing trunks if I knew that in advance!” said the cheeky Matthew with a glint in his eye. The Major accepted the humour at his expense. It was a good disguise for the nerves the men were no doubt feeling as they neared their target.

As the car reached the top of Roseworthy Hill the Major pulled over into a lay-by that led to a field entrance on the right . He then let the car roll back between two hedges so it was hidden from view except from the front.

"What's this place?" asked Matthew.

"This is the old original road before the turnpike trust built the new, more gentle hill out of Roseworthy," explained the Major. "However, it is the ideal spot for you to get hidden before we run into the roadblocks the other side of Connor Downs. We'll meet the first pillbox as we drop down Carwin Rise before we get to Hayle."

The four men clambered out of the car. Three of them stretched knowing it would be a while before they would feel comfortable again. The Major went round and opened the boot.

Chapter Three

"Your papers certainly seem in order, Mr van…" Mrs Browning's voice trailed away as she was uncertain as to how to pronounce the name on the identity card in front of her.

"Oh please, just call me Johann. That's easier to say than a Dutch surname."

"As you wish, but I don't like getting too familiar with my lodgers." Mrs Browning looked the young man up and down and handed back the identity card and various permits. Johann silently gave a sigh of relief. The boys at 76 Tirpitzufer had done their job. He just hoped they would stand up to scrutiny when he came into contact with the authorities.

"You are happy with the room?" his new landlady asked. Johann glanced around the first floor room of the terraced house in Bar Road. It had a bed, a chair, a table with a wash bowl and jug on it, and a chest of drawers. More importantly, it had a view across Falmouth harbour so he could keep an eye on the comings and goings of the vessels that used the southern wharves.

"And you're happy with the price?" The questions kept coming. Johann said that he was. The cash he'd been supplied with for the mission would easily cover it. He could have stayed in one of Falmouth's famous hotels, but he didn't want the added scrutiny or the attentions of other guests, so a humble room by a couple that didn't want to take in evacuees would suffice for the couple of months he intended to be here.

“So you are going to be working at the docks, you say,” said Mrs Browning.

“I hope so. I worked at the docks in Rotterdam before the…, you know,” Johann lied.

“Yes, it must have been awful to have your country overrun by those Germans. Still, we’ve got a number of your countrymen here. The paper the other day had a photo of Dutch cadets training at a house not far from Falmouth. Who knows, you might even be able to meet them.” Mrs Browning’s suggestion filled Johann with horror. The last thing he needed was someone exposing his false identity. Of all the places in Britain, why would the Dutch choose Falmouth?

“That would be lovely,” he said smiling. “Although I think it unlikely as I shall be busy working long shifts at the dockyard.”

“Yes, that will certainly be the case. My brother is a chargehand there and he does long, long days. I’ll show you where the key is should you get back after I’ve locked the front door for the night. You can let yourself in. But no guests in the room after 8 o’clock, and no lady friends in the room at any time. I don’t keep an unruly house, Mr Johann.”

“You need not worry about me,” Johann said. “I will be concentrating on the job I came here to do.”

“Very well then. And you are certain you don’t need meals provided? Because if you do, I’ll need your ration book.” Johann felt Mrs Browning was hoping to gain by having the extra card.

"No," he said. "As long as I can make a cup of coffee when I need one, I shall be fine."

"Coffee!" she exclaimed. "What do you think this is, the Pentargon Hotel? There's a kettle by the stove and some tea in the caddy, but don't you go using it all up. I'll need your coupons if I am to get you your weekly two ounces."

"Tea is rationed?" asked Johann. That had changed since he was in Cornwall last.

"Oh yes. We don't grow it in this country so our ships have to bring it in. Been rationed since July last year. Where have you been if you didn't know that?"

Johann ignored the question, opened his ration book and went to tear out the tea pages.

"What on earth are you doing?" said Mrs Browning in amazement. "I'll need to take the whole book to the shop I am registered with in order to get your tea."

"Oh," said Johann wondering how he would be able to feed himself whilst carrying out his mission.

"Just leave it with me on a Thursday and I'll get you the weekly ration," said Mrs Browning much to Johann's relief.

"That will be most helpful," said Johann not relishing the prospect of leaving any of his documents with his landlady. Certainly a detail he'd have to report back to his superiors at Abwehr II.

"Well, I'll leave you to unpack your things and get yourself settled in," said Mrs Browning stepping towards the door. "You can pay me the first week when you've got yourself sorted. I'll be downstairs in the kitchen." Johann closed the door behind her and sat down on the bed. The first of the day's tasks was done.

"Your papers certainly seem in order. General labour is what you'll start as. If you show an aptitude for a certain type of work and an opening comes you may then be able to specialise, but general labour will help give you the feel of the place and what we expect of our workers. The standards here are high. It is important war work that we are engaged in." The voice belonged to Mr Pearn. He was one of the managers for Silley, Cox and Co (Engineers) Ltd, the company that did the repair work on the ships at Falmouth Docks. The running of the docks was in the hands of another of the family's concerns, the Falmouth Docks Company. John Silley, the Chief Director, who had purchased the Falmouth concerns in 1918 and had overseen much development in the port and its facilities in the intervening years, had died suddenly at his Port Navas home in January and the various companies were now in the hands of his two sons. Mr Pearn interviewed all of the permanent employees, a personal touch that the company was noted for. Indeed, John Silley was known to have conversed freely with his workforce and had been a generous benefactor to the town of Falmouth, helping mould the plans for worker's housing in the garden village of Swanvale, building 24 pensioner's homes in Theydon Road and donating them to the Council and buying the X-ray apparatus for the Falmouth & District Hospital.

"Work hard, follow instructions, and you will get on fine," Mr Pearn continued. "Be at the gate at seven thirty sharp tomorrow morning and ask for Mr Matthews. He will sort you out from there." Mr Pearn stood up, shook Johann's hand and that was it. As he headed back to the dockyard gate, Johann couldn't believe how well things were going. He was now a dock labourer. The second of the day's tasks was done.

"Your papers are not in order." Johann smarted at the challenge and looked down at the documents he held in his hand.

"See, that's what will give you away. You must have complete confidence. A policeman or security guard will sense your fear. You need to say without blinking an eye, 'What could possibly be wrong with my papers?' The British think they rule the world and so would bluster their way through any such confrontation. The papers are good. You must be too."

Johann looked at the formidable woman. He didn't know what to say. He had expected a clandestine meeting with his Fifth Column contact, not an interrogation covering all the details of his current life in Cornwall. At least she seemed satisfied with his lodging arrangements and was positively pleased by his securing employment within the dockyard, but he was grateful she was an ally and not the enemy.

"Now put them away before we arouse suspicion," she said looking around. The two of them were sat on a bench in the Kimberley Park gardens. The flower beds were full of spring colour but there weren't many people in the park on this sunny May afternoon.

"I shall be here every Sunday at two o'clock so you can pass on any messages then," she said. "But make sure you are not followed before coming into the park."

"I am not an amateur," protested Johann at her inference. "How do I contact you if there is an emergency?" he asked. She took a piece of paper out of her handbag.

"This," she said, "Is my address and telephone number. Read it. Memorise it and then destroy it. You must only use it if the mission is totally lost or when you have completed it successfully and are ready to leave."

"How will you call my pick up? Do you have wireless contact with our forces?" Johann asked.

"The less you know about my husband and I and how we operate the better. Then you can't reveal it under interrogation. All you need know is when your mission is done we will have your transport within 48 hours," she said in hushed tones.

"Where is this haven?" Johann asked looking at the piece of paper.

"It's about fifteen miles east of here. It's a small fishing village on the south coast," she explained. "Now I must be going. I have a short walk to catch my train to Truro. Good luck. Take care. The British execute spies." She paused as she saw the look on Johann's face. "Oh yes, when they executed two last December it was in all the papers." She stood up, put her hand on his knee. “For the Fatherland,” she said bringing their focus back to the reason Johann was here and before he had chance to reply she was walking away at a brisk pace. He sighed. The third and last of the day’s tasks was done.

Chapter Four

The Major braked as the soldier stepped out into the road and raised his right hand. Another infantryman stood at the side of the road covering the first with his rifle. The Major pulled up two feet from the corporal and wound down his window. The soldier came round the front of the car, saluted and then said,

"Your papers, please sir." The Major handed over his Identity Card and his military pass that gave him 'access to all areas in Cornwall'. It was the first time the soldier had seen such a document and he turned it over and back and then read the front again.

"You know where you're heading, sir?" the soldier asked.

"Oh yes, thank you," the Major replied. He decided the soldier was taking too much of an interest and to distract him said,

"That's some fancy pillbox you've got there, corporal," nodding towards the garage on the right hand side of the road. The concrete block pillbox had been covered in a wooden shed with a corrugated iron roof and made to look like a small petrol filling station complete with enamel plates advertising Dunlop Tyres, BP Motor Spirit and Lyons Tea. The soldier turned to admire the masterpiece.

"Yes sir, she's looking good. Hopefully will fool the Hun until he gets hit by our withering fire," the corporal replied. The Major reached out his hand for his papers and said,

“Well, I’ll leave you to sell your Lyons Tea and be on my way.”

“Yes, sir,” said the corporal handing back the documents. He stood to attention and saluted as the Major gently put his foot on the accelerator and the Snipe pulled away. When he was a safe distance a way he said in a loud voice to his passengers,

“First one done. We should be ok now until we get to the bridge before the power station. Be there in five minutes.”

“Very good, sir,” said Daniel in muffled tones from under the floor rug in the back. There was no comment from Ken and Matthew in the boot.

The Major drove through Copperhouse, slowing only once to let a woman cross the road with her child in a perambulator. As he approached St Elwyn’s Church he slowed ready to turn right onto the swing bridge. On the right opposite the church hall was an emergency water tank. Its purpose was to supply the fire brigade in case of an air raid. By the swing bridge, built to carry both road and rail across the channel that fed Copperhouse Pool, there was another roadblock. The Major pulled up in front of it and wound his window down again. He decided he would be more proactive this time.

“Major Trevennel with an appointment at two o’clock at the power station. I’m running a little late so I’d be grateful if you could get that thing shifted quickly,” he said to the soldier who approached the car. When the private saw the rank, he immediately responded,

“Yes sir, of course, sir,” and shouted to his two companions to lift the red and white painted pole out of its seat in the X shaped supports. As soon as it was clear he waved the Major through. As he drove across the bridge, the Major noted that demolition charges were set for the bridge to be blown in the event of an invasion.

He drove past the Custom House, past the public house and onto North Quay smiling to himself that there was one last check point to get his passengers through. The Major went past a stone shed on the left and then kept to the left of the wall that took the railway line inside the British Ethyl Corporation’s bromine plant. Soldiers guarded the entrance. They watched him pass but did nothing to impede his progress. The plant had been built in 1939 by Imperial Chemicals Industries under orders from the government to provide the UK with a source of bromine anti-knock agent. The bromine was extracted from the sea water. Prior to the war the RAF relied on imported lead anti-knock additives, but Hayle with its remote location but plentiful supply of sea water and good rail links and power station became Britain’s sole source of bromine. The Major spotted there were anti-aircraft guns and look-out posts on the roof of its tallest building. Out in the harbour he could see there were booms which prevented vessels from approaching the quay. Fortunately the Germans had not yet bombed the plant allowing it to produce 579 tons of bromine last year making a vital contribution to the RAF’s performance in the Battle of Britain and for the planes of Bomber Command now taking the war to the enemy.

The Major's stomach tightened as he saw the coal-carrying gantry and turned to the right and viewed the gates of the power station ahead. Two soldiers stood behind the closed gates. He drew the car up to the gates, stopped and got out of the car. The soldiers on seeing the vastly superior rank saluted.

"Major Trevennel to see Mr Peller and your commanding officer. They are expecting me," the Major said matter of factly.

"May we see your papers please, sir?" the tallest of the two soldiers asked. The Major handed the two documents through the gate. As the soldier examined them the Major looked along the perimeter. Upright concrete posts held a netted wire fence topped by a strand of barbed wire. At the top the posts sloped inwards with three more strands of barbed wire making climbing the fence much more difficult. He thought that his ruse was certainly the easiest way of getting his men inside.

"All correct, sir," said the soldier handing back the papers. "Open the gate, Geoff," he said to one of his colleagues. The Major returned to the car, waited until the gate was fully open and then drove slowly inside. He went past a small building on the right and then saw that there were a few vehicles parked against a retaining wall. There was a three ton army truck, a motorcycle and sidecar painted in its customary olive green and then a couple of civilian cars, which he assumed belonged to the power station managers. Ignoring the first gap the Major pulled up to the end of the line and reverse parked against the wall making sure he left enough room for his passengers to ease out of the boot.

“Stay down,” he hissed at Daniel. “One of the soldiers is approaching.” The Major got out of the car to meet him.

“I’ll show you to Mr Peller’s office, sir.” It was the soldier who had checked his papers.

“Excellent, private,” the Major said, and with a quick glance back at the car to make sure nothing was giving the game away, he followed the soldier along the roadway past some of the sheds he’d told his men about and between the turbine hall and transformer building. Partway along they turned to the right and mounted a flight of steps towards a door. A soldier stood on duty at the top of the steps. When he saw the Major he stood to attention and saluted.

“At ease,” the Major barked and his guide nodded to the sentry to open the door. It wasn’t locked, he just turned the handle and let the two men past. The Major wondered how many more sentries were posted about the place. Inside he was guided up a flight of stairs with handrails on both sides. He was led past the control room which had another soldier stood outside the door, and to an office just adjacent. The soldier knocked the door, waited for permission to enter and then showed the Major in.

The office was not unlike the one he’d been in a few hours previously at Carn Brea. Obviously the company bought its furniture in job lots. It was smaller than the Central Office, but the same table, chairs, light and telephone gave the Major a sense of déjà vu. The gentleman behind the desk stood up. He was probably mid to late fifties with a balding head, greying hair and large eyebrows. His cheek bones were set high but his face seemed friendly. He wore a stiff collar and had a white handkerchief protruding from the pocket of his jacket.

"Alfred Peller, Superintendent, pleased to meet you," he said holding out his hand. The Major shook it and introduced himself.

"And this is Second Lieutenant Oldroyd, the officer commanding the detachment of troops here in Hayle guarding the North Quay installations," Mr Peller continued. The officer saluted; the Major returned the salute.

"Please be seated, gentlemen," said Mr Peller seating himself at his desk. The officers took off their caps and sat themselves down on the hardbacked chairs in front of the desk.

"What can we do for you, Major?" said Mr Peller.

"I'll come straight to the point. With the prospect of an invasion imminent as the weather improves, we need to be ever vigilant against any activity that the enemy may engage in. I don't need to explain to you how vital this power station is, not only to the plant next door, but also to the mines and industry and military installations in the whole of Cornwall, not just the Hayle area. Thus I have ordered an exercise that will test your security measures over the next couple of days. Both the guards and the civilian employees must be vigilant in order that the security and performance of the station is not compromised." The Major paused to let the import of his words sink in. Oldroyd took the opportunity to dive in with a question.

"Just what form will this exercise take? Are we to expect a company landing on the beach?"

“It could be, though the minefield would prevent a full on frontal assault,” replied the Major letting the officer know he knew about the defences around Hayle. But he wasn’t going to let him off so easily.

“It may be parachutists that land on the Quay. When the Germans captured the impregnable Belgian fort of Eben Emael last May they landed ten gliders right on top of the fort.” Second Lieutenant Oldroyd’s face was a picture as he imagined such a scenario on Hayle’s North Quay. The Major continued.

“Equally it could be a group of saboteurs or a Fifth Columnist amongst the workforce,” he teased hoping to make Mr Peller realise that his employees could be the weak link.

“At two o’clock tomorrow afternoon I shall carry out a full inspection of the power station and I trust I will find that its plant and machinery are intact and its perimeter is still secure in the hands of the West Yorkshire Regiment. Is that understood?”

“Yes sir,” chimed the officer. Mr Peller looked somewhat bemused but nodded as it seemed the right thing to do.

I’ll see you at two tomorrow gentlemen,” said the Major standing up and putting on his cap. “I’ll see myself out.” He gently closed the door behind him and headed for the stairs. Halfway down he paused and looked at his watch. He hoped he had given his men enough time to get clear from the car and find cover. Outside the door he lingered a little longer asking the sentry about his duties, his billet and his regiment’s reception in the town of Hayle. The answers were all positive and when the

Major could spin it out no longer without raising suspicion he took his leave and headed back to the car.

He glanced in the rear passenger window and there was no sign of Daniel under the rug. He went round to the boot and noticed while it had been put in the closed position it wasn't actually shut. The men had extradited themselves but didn't want to make any noise that would draw attention so hadn't shut it. The Major did so, climbed in the driver's seat, started the ignition and with an extra rev of the engine to let his men know he was going, pulled away towards the gate. He wished his men luck as the sentry opened the gate, and then wished himself luck for his mission that evening as he pulled away along North Quay and headed back towards the A30.

Chapter Five

Elizabeth was leaning over the sink pouring a jug of water over her hair when Bunny stuck her head round the door and said,

"Sergeant Buscombe wants to see you in her office."

"Oh Bunny be a dear and tell her I shall be at least ten minutes while I finish washing my hair. It's the first chance I've had to get all the dust out since I was caught up in that beastly air raid," Elizabeth said putting the jug down and reaching for the 6d sachet of Amami No 5 shampoo.

"I thought Friday night was Amami night," said Bunny with a grin.

"I was lucky to get any shampoo at all and in this place Amami night is whenever you can snatch a few moments to yourself! Please do tell her, you know what she can be like."

"As it's you, I will," said Bunny sighing deeply for exaggerated effect. "But you don't want to keep her waiting too long!" she added as she disappeared from sight. Elizabeth wondered what Sergeant Buscombe wanted this time of the evening as she worked the shampoo into a lather and rubbed her scalp hard and then rubbed her long flowing blonde hair. It was rare these days to see it at its full length; usually it was tied up at the back of the head but having it cut short was an option Elizabeth had resisted all the while she had been in the Auxiliary Territorial Service. She then rinsed it in cold water, pouring several jugfuls over it to do so. Finally she took a large towel and wrapped her hair into it and tied it up on her head. Drying it properly could wait until she had seen what her superior wanted. She buttoned up her khaki shirt, pulled on her tunic and headed for the door.

Her hand reached for the handle on the door of Sergeant Buscombe's office but stopped. Elizabeth decided she'd better knock before barging in. She tapped on the door, turned the handle and stepped in.

"I'm sorry to keep you waiting, Ma'am but as you can see I was in the middle of washing one's hair and was not in a fit state to come immediately," said Elizabeth thinking it would be prudent to get her apology in before there was any criticism of the time it took for her to respond to her summons. Sergeant Buscombe looked up from her desk. Her face did not appear angry.

"It's not me you have kept waiting, corporal," she said nodding towards the chair that was screened by the open door. Elizabeth peered round the door and exclaimed,

"Zac!" and gave him a great big hug as he stood up. Sergeant Buscombe coughed and pronounced,

"That's Major Trevennel to you in this office."

"I am so sorry, sergeant," Elizabeth replied quickly. "I am sorry too, Major. But it was such a surprise." She then became conscious of the Major taking in her unusual headgear. She put her hands to her head and blurted out,

"I am so sorry I am not suitably dressed. You have caught me unawares. What are you doing here?"

The Major calmly said, "Sergeant Buscombe has given me permission to take you out of barracks for an hour." Elizabeth turned to see her sergeant sitting back in her chair with her arms crossed. It was obvious she wasn't entirely approving but rank had pulled its weight and there was little the sergeant could do faced with a determined and persuasive Major.

"It is not normal procedure, Corporal Treluckey," said Sergeant Buscombe, "But you have had a bagful of it lately and I've agreed to the Major's request on this occasion. Now go and rub that hair dry. Don't let the damp get into you. The Major will wait for you here."

"Yes ma'am. Thank you ma'am." Elizabeth wheeled about and headed out the door. Her head was in a spin and her heart was all aflutter. Back in the dormitory she rubbed her hair with the towel and brushed it out starting from the bottom to the top to get any tangles out. Normally this would take ages and be done sat in front of a mirror, but tonight it was all over in five minutes. A quick dab of the Californian Poppy perfume she had bought from Woolworths and she was ready. 'Better to have the time with Zac,' she thought, 'Than to waste it trying to look perfect.'

The Major thought she looked perfect and told her so as they walked down St Nicholas Street. Elizabeth swelled with pride and joy. She kept looking at the Major, handsome, athletically built, and couldn't believe it was really him on her arm.

"So to what do I owe this unexpected surprise?" she asked. "And how did you talk Sergeant Buscombe into letting me out?"

"I have a little work to do in Cornwall. I expect to be here for a fortnight." Elizabeth's heart skipped for joy at the prospect of finding some time with the Major in between his duties. "And as for Sergeant Buscombe, she talked herself into it. I had merely asked to see you for ten minutes, but she then told me how you were at St Eval on Monday when it was badly bombed and had wondered if she should give you leave but decided keeping you busy was the best way to help you get over it. So when she said my unannounced arrival would be a special fillip for you, I suggested we made it worth my while by taking you out for a drink. However, she restricted it to an hour."

"Oh you are wonderful. It is so good to see you."

"Let's go in here for a drink," said the Major as they approached the George & Dragon at the bottom of St Nicholas Street. "We can get a drink here and save time walking up into Fore Street." Elizabeth had always thought the three storey public house had a bit of a reputation from the comments the ATS girls made but decided the Major's suggestion was a good one as time was so precious. So she agreed, confident that his presence would protect her, and they headed in through the door.

The ceiling was low and the Major naturally stooped as he led her to the bar. With drinks in hand they found a small table over in the corner. One or two of the regulars were raising an eyebrow at a major deigning to grace them with his presence but nothing was said that the couple picked up on. They only had eyes for each other. The first ten minutes were spent catching up on each other's news since their last exchange of letters, or at least that news which they were happy to divulge in a public house. 'Keep mum – she's not so dumb' said the poster pinned above the bar. Then the Major's expression changed.

"Elizabeth, the real reason for coming to see you this evening…" Elizabeth fixed her eyes on his wondering what was coming next. "…Is to ask whether you would come and visit my parents for the weekend? I've arranged work so that I am free and would love to take you to meet them and to show you Bosvarren."

"That sounds so lovely, but how do I persuade Sergeant Buscombe? I'm in the army, you know, I can't just swan off for the weekend when I choose," said Elizabeth with a note of exasperation in her voice. How her heart so longed for a weekend with her beloved, but her head knew that duty must come first.

"I was telling you how Sergeant Buscombe talked herself into giving you time off," said the Major with a glint in his eye. "Well, I only told you part of the story. The bit I missed out was I suggested she gave you a weekend pass, and she agreed. When I then asked to break the news to you myself if you agreed to my request, that was when she then restricted us to an hour, because she has given you from twelve hundred hours on Friday to nineteen hundred hours on Sunday. Forty eight hours plus travel."

“Oh Zac, how did you manage that? That is wonderful. I know I missed out on my weekend home last month because there was a bit of a flap on, but I didn’t expect to get a forty eight hour pass this weekend. You are spiffing.”

“So you’ll come with me to Bosvarren?” asked the Major.

“Of course I will. I will be delighted,” Elizabeth replied, both excited at the prospect of meeting his parents as she felt it showed he was serious about their friendship but terrified at the potential pitfalls of failing to meet parental expectations.

“That’s settled, then,” said the Major with a sense of achievement that his mission for the night was accomplished. “I will pick you up at twelve hundred Friday. I have a meeting Friday afternoon with someone at the Docks in Falmouth, but I am sure you can amuse yourself in the shops for an hour. I will telephone mother and let her know we’ll be there in time for tea.” The Major downed the rest of his drink. “Now let’s get you back to barracks on time, and I have a two hour’s drive ahead of me.” They made their way out of the public house watched by every eye in the bar as people wondering who the film star couple in uniform were. Arm in arm they walked back up the street, the Major singing “The night has music, the sweetest music” as he serenaded Elizabeth with some lines from the latest Vera Lynn tune. They continued past the station and to the barracks where the Major said goodbye at the gate to the Keep as he had left his car in the road alongside the barrack wall. He stood and watched as the sentry let Elizabeth through the gate and returned to the car a happy man.

Chapter Six

The Major was satisfied with his morning's work as he drove his car along the coast road through Gwithian towards Hayle. He had spent the morning inspecting the anti-invasion measures at Portreath which had gained a greater significance since the RAF had opened their new sector aerodrome on the farmland above the village at Nancekuke. The small village had a harbour into which coal from the South Wales coalfields was brought for the mines in the Camborne and Redruth area. He had been shown the dragon's teeth on the ramp at Smuggler's Cove, the scaffolding that crossed the beach, the pillboxes, one on the slope behind Battery House, the other next to Smuggler's Cottage, and the vast anti-tank wall that surrounded the exit from the beach and the harbour. He had seen how some of the exits from the harbour had been blocked off with concrete block walls, like the steps up to Harbour Terrace and the trackway behind its row of cottages. He had heard how the tracks on the 1837 incline of the Portreath Branch Line had been lifted in August last year and an anti-tank wall built across the incline just above the bridge over Glenfeadon Terrace. The Major was impressed there was a second line of defence at the landward end of the village with anti-tank walls across the track behind the school through the woods to Illogan and across the road along the valley to Redruth and even further up the valley there were roadblocks at Laity and Cambrose. With the anti-aircraft batteries dotted around the airfield and up on the cliffs at Carvannel Downs he felt all that could reasonably be done to protect Portreath from invasion had been done.

As he came to the pillboxes either side of the road at Upton Towans he had to produce his papers for the roadblock. He was quickly through and on his way dropping down the hill to Loggans Mill. It was twelve thirty. He would just have time for some lunch in Copperhouse before returning to the Power Station.

At ten to two he was driving over the swing bridge and onto North Quay suitably refreshed and ready for an interesting afternoon. As he drove along the quay road he noticed there were extra patrolling soldiers on the quayside and at the entrance to the bromine works and as he approached the gates of the power station there were four soldiers on duty instead of yesterday's two. The Major smiled to himself thinking 'I'm glad they took the need for vigilance seriously.' He was soon through the gate and parked and being escorted to Mr Peller's office. Second Lieutenant Oldroyd was already there which pleased the Major. He felt it was a sign the young officer had taken the exercise seriously.

"Good afternoon gentlemen," said the Major as he entered carrying a kit bag in one hand and his baton in the other. The two men stood up and Oldroyd saluted. The Major duly acknowledged and then said,

"I would like a full guided tour of the power station from both of you. Let's begin in the turbine hall."

Mr Peller led the way followed by the Major with Oldroyd trailing behind. The turbine hall was a huge voluminous building with the turbines and plant that fed them spaced along the middle. At various points it seemed the floor was cut away as steps and walkways provided access to the machinery at different levels. It didn't take the Major long to spot one of the dummy limpet mines. With the baton he had brought along expressly for the purpose he pointed to it stuck on the casing of the turbine and looking at the Yorkshire officer said,

"What's that?" Oldroyd did a double take and said,

"I'm not quite sure what this is, sir." Then as he peered a little closer added, "It looks to me like an explosive charge."

"Take it off and put it in the bag," said the Major handing him the kitbag. Oldroyd gingerly fingered the limpet mine, pulled and was amazed it was held in place by a magnet. He turned it over and was mightily relieved to read the word 'Dummy' on the underside. He dropped it into the bag and the party moved on. The Major stopped by a large pipe that rose vertically and then turned ninety degrees to go out through the wall at about fifteen feet above the wall. It brought the high pressure steam into the turbine to turn the blades.

"What's this?"

"It looks like another one, sir," said Oldroyd. Peller looked aghast. The Major found a further four in the turbine hall, some at crucial valves and one on a panel of gauges. He then indicated they should go into the furnace building and as he led the way down the long turbine hall he could hear the whispered conversation behind him.

"You told me that the perimeter was secure all the time and that there was no breach." The voice was Mr Peller's.

"There wasn't. I am sure of that. Perhaps you have got a Fifth Columnist working here." It was Oldroyd throwing the accusation of responsibility back at the station superintendant. The Major smiled and kept walking. He was going to enjoy the next thirty minutes. His Auxiliary Unit guys had obviously done a good job.

In the furnace plant they found three more including one on the huge boiler. Mr Peller was horrified. Oldroyd was getting more and more nervous. As the Major's confidence in how well his 'saboteurs' had done grew, he said,

"Let's go to the transformer building." He let Mr Peller lead the way. The Major was keeping his eyes peeled for his men. He was sure they would be hidden somewhere so they could enjoy the moment. However, he didn't spot a thing.

On the huge transformers they found a further six charges. The exasperated Oldroyd was now carrying the kitbag over one shoulder. He was appalled that such a breach of security had obviously taken place on his watch. He expected to be severely punished. The Major asked to be taken down into the tunnel where the huge high voltage cables left the building. They found a further four limpet mines.

"I think we should finish up with a visit to the control room," said the triumphant Major. Mr Peller's face was white; Second Lieutenant Oldroyd's was red. The Major followed them up the steps past the guard on the door, up the staircase to the guard outside the control room. Mr Peller led the way inside. A single operative sat at the control desk monitoring the vast array of gauges and panels of switches in front of him. To everyone's horror the Major found three limpet mines attached to different control panels. By his reckoning he had found all but one of the dummy limpet mines. He decided he would leave that as a reminder of the exercise to be discovered at some future point.

"Let's reconvene in your office, Mr Peller," the Major said and the crestfallen superintendant led the way across the landing to his office. The Major was the last to enter and he closed the door behind him.

"Well gentlemen, it looks to me as if this plant would have been rendered totally inoperative had those charges been real." Oldroyd could picture the court martial summons. Peller wondered if central office would demand his resignation and whether he should do the honourable thing and offer it first. The Major continued,

"I trust this exercise has brought home that vigilance is an every minute, every hour, every day thing. You cannot switch it off for a second because that's when the enemy will strike. Your security is as good as your least alert soldier, your least observant employee, and I think I have shown that both of you have some considerable work to do to improve the performance of the men you are responsible for." The two men meekly acknowledged that there was. The Major's next comment took them completely by surprise.

"Now I am not here to get anyone into trouble. I will take no further action. You say nothing about today's event outside this plant and I'll say nothing about it to your superiors. But you've hopefully learned your lesson."

"But how on earth did your men get into the power station?" blurted out Oldroyd, half out of relief and half out of wanting to know the worst.

"For me to know and you to wonder," said the Major teasing, not that the two mightily relieved men realised it. "Now perhaps you could show me to my car." The two men accompanied the Major down the stairs exchanging quizzical looks with each other to see if the other had any clue. As they reached the car the Major looked around and there was still no sign of his men. He took the kitbag from Oldroyd and went to the boot, opened it and said,

"Alright you can come out now and travel home in comfort." To the amazement of Mr Peller and Second Lieutenant Oldroyd two men clambered out of the boot while a third appeared in the footwell of the back seat.

"Vigilance is an every minute, every hour, every day thing. It doesn't start when an exercise starts. It doesn't start when the balloon goes up. Remember that, and you'll have learned your lesson." With that he got into the driver's seat, started the engine and with his passengers aboard pulled away towards the gate. The sentries had opened them by the time the car reached the entrance when Daniel in the front seat yelled,

"Stop! Stop!" The Major hit the breaks and the car stopped with a squeal. He looked at Daniel wondering what the problem was. Daniel wound down his window, beckoned to one of the sentries and as he came over said,

“Excuse me mate, could we have our limpet mine back?” He pointed to the charge stuck on the back of a metal sign in the middle of the gate.” The soldier looked both horrified and perplexed but did as he was instructed. The Major couldn’t help laughing as he pulled away.

“How on earth did you manage that one?” he asked.

“We’ll tell you, but we think you owe us a pint first,” said Matthew grinning from ear to ear. It was obvious the men had had a thoroughly enjoyable and successful time.

Two hours later at ten to six the men were sat in the car outside the Lanivet Inn on the A30 waiting for it to open. The whitewashed building had the Lanivet part of its name blacked out so its sign above the door now read “The … Inn.” Next door at the village shop where its standout lettering above the windows of the flat over the shop usually read ‘Lanivet Supply Stores’ the place name was now covered over with a sheet of plywood. This was all to make sure that the Germans didn’t know where they were when they stopped for a loaf of bread or a pint of Cornish ale.

“As soon as it opens, I’ll buy you the promised pint. You can see we’ve stopped to go in, now tell me how you did it all at the power station.” The Major was both quite exasperated and impressed that the men had maintained their silence on the subject since they had left Hayle.

“Take the keys off him, Daniel,” said Ken from the back seat.

"You lot drive a hard bargain," said the Major handing them over. "Now tell me before we get inside and there are too many listening ears."

"When you left us in the car," began Daniel, "I made sure all was clear and then helped the other two out of the boot. Just a few yards away was a shed so we dived in there. It was unlocked and was obviously the garden shed. It had a lawnmower, wheelbarrow and various tools and in the back was a toilet. We made a small sign 'Out Of Order' scratched on a piece of wood with a screwdriver and put it on the lavatory door. That was our bolt hole in case anyone came. We only used it once, just before the shift change over, someone headed towards the shed and so we all went in the toilet and locked the door. He came in the shed, put something down and then tried the toilet door, obviously then saw the sign, grunted and went away again. He didn't lock the shed door.

"We had devised a plan on who would go where. As it was getting dark we started to do a few recce runs to harden up the planning. The transformer building with the control room in it was the most heavily guarded so we decided we would do the rest of the power station first and then if all went well meet back at the shed to then tackle the biggest challenge."

"I did the furnace and boiler building," said Matthew. "It was easy. There was so much noise from what was going on I had plenty of cover. Just timing my runs from here to there I was able to avoid the power station workers. I must have seen about six of them but they were all intent on their tasks they caused me no concern."

"Daniel and I did the turbine building," said Ken. "There were about four workers in there. We got in no problem at the south end and just giving each other the nod when it was clear worked our way along the turbine hall."

"You should have seen Mr Peller's face when I pointed out the limpet mine on the high pressure steam pipe," said the Major keen to impress on the men how good a job they had done. The Major doubted if regular troops could have carried out such a job, but that's why he chose Auxiliary Unit lads. They were used to moving by stealth in the shadows.

"So we met back up at the shed and decided the guard at the door by the steps needed distracting," Daniel continued the story. "That's when Matthew helped us out. He does a wonderful cat impression." Matthew duly gave the Major a rendition of his mournful meowing. "It got the guard's attention but he wasn't leaving his post. So Matthew found a dustbin lid from somewhere and with a combination of cat noises dropped the lid with what to us seemed like an enormous clatter. That brought the guard down the steps and round the corner."

"I'd fled out of sight before he got there," interjected Matthew.

"It was long enough for Ken and myself to sprint up the steps, get through the door and close it quietly behind us," continued Daniel. "Ken stayed downstairs and went for the transformers. I crept up the stairs towards the control room. Halfway up I could see the helmet of a guard outside the door. I was wondering what to do, couldn't see a way past him and was on the point of retreating down the stairs to find Ken, when the guard felt the call of nature and went to relieve himself. I seized the opportunity and made it into the control room."

"But what about the operative sat at the desk?" asked the Major.

"He was reading a newspaper and so didn't notice me enter. I ducked down and crawled behind the bank of instrument panels on the long desk he was sat at. I crawled along placing one on the back of his desk, and one on the panel that had lots of dials grouped together in threes. At this point I was only about three feet from him."

"He still didn't notice?" asked the incredulous Major.

"No. There's a low hum, I guess from all the equipment. At one point he looked up from his paper, pulled open a drawer in his desk somewhere and took out a sandwich and began eating it. After a quick glance across all the panels in front of him to see that the dials and gauges were reading as they should he continued reading his paper. I continued crawling out from behind the far end of the control desk and looped round behind the table that was a few feet behind his chair and made for the door. I stood up, opened it and shut it quickly, said to the startled guard 'All clear in there,' and scurried down the stairs before he had time to answer."

"So how did you get back out past the guard on the entrance?" asked the Major.

"We didn't," said Ken. "I had found a back door to the building that was both unlocked and unguarded so we accepted their kind provision and used that."

"I reckon there's going to be lots of red faces and sheepish people when Peller and Oldroyd review the exercise with their respective men," said the Major delighted that the penetration of the plant had been complete. The Major knew it held out hope for specially trained men to be able to penetrate some of the enemy held installations that Churchill was keen to send the Commando and the agents of the Special Operations Executive to deal with.

"But what about the one on the gate. That was priceless," said the Major.

"That was me," piped up Matthew. "Having distracted the guard I had gone onto the grass bank up behind the sheds and where you parked the car, and in the black out was able to get down towards the gate. When the sentry who had investigated my dustbin lid returned to the bottom of the steps the men on the gate had walked partway towards him to find out what was happening and that gave me enough time to stick the limpet on the metal sign and scurry back up behind the sheds."

"We then hid back in the shed, having to use the 'Out Of Order' ruse twice during today, before we saw you return and then when it was all clear made our way back into the car," Daniel concluded the account with a grin that showed a high degree of satisfaction.

"An absolutely marvellous job," said the Major knowing Churchill would enjoy hearing the account, even if he fumed at the incompetence of the defenders. But that was what this mission was designed to highlight and to bring Britain back to a heightened state of alert as the prospect of invasion again reared its head. A full onslaught across the Channel would be obvious but the unseen enemy operating in diverse places around the country required the vigilance of every citizen and that is what the Prime Minister wanted to achieve.

"Well, you have more than deserved that pint," said the Major noticing the landlord had unlocked the front door. "Come on, let's drink to your success."

Chapter Seven

There were two happy occupants of the car as it made its way along Wood Lane leaving the town of Falmouth behind. Elizabeth had spent a happy hour window shopping, admiring some wonderful outfits but sighing as she knew she couldn't afford the price on most of them. 'Maybe one day,' she dreamed, 'The Major would treat her to a new dress.' For now though, what she had packed in her small case for the weekend would have to suffice and she had consoled herself with a cup of tea and a biscuit in a little tea room over one of the shops. She had sat by the window that overlooked the harbour and wondered just what the Major was up to in the docks.

The Major was pleased that his meeting with Dunstan of the Security Service had gone well. Dunstan was part of a small team that was working under the auspices of MI5 on port security, vetting the crews of every vessel entering and leaving the port. Wearing a uniform that declared him to be 'Port Security Police', Bob, as he introduced himself, had been able to give the Major a good appraisal on the security of the harbour. Their meeting had taken place in the old Victorian chapel of the British Sailor's Society which they were using as their headquarters. Known as the 'Seamen's Bethel' they had sat below the huge pulpit complete with ship's wheel. Originally it had been shaped like a ship's bow but had been modified in the rebuilding done in 1893. Lifebelts from the Mohegan which had been wrecked on the Manacles in October 1898 hung on the wall. They had helped save some 44 souls, although 106 were lost in a disaster caused by human error.

The Major had learned first-hand Bob's role in the apprehension of a radio officer aboard a Norwegian ship in the harbour who was thought to be communicating with an enemy submarine in the waters outside the harbour. They had boarded the vessel using a naval picket boat and an unarmed Bob, backed up by a naval officer and a rating both armed, had descended below deck to collect the man despite the vain protests of the ship's captain. Bob recalled, although he doesn't suffer from seasickness, the foot odour that permeated the tiny cabin, made the arrest memorable. How the Major had laughed.

They had discussed petty thieving by dock workers, the risk of sabotage and strike, and just who had prior knowledge of ship movements. They had agreed that the anti-aircraft cover had been woefully lacking after the fall of France, but Bob had said things were vastly improved now with the provision of the ring of anti-aircraft batteries and the balloon barrage. Bob had said the defence of the harbour seaward was a naval matter but the booms seemed to be working well and the provision of guns and searchlights around the harbour was improving all the time. Landward the Worcestershire Line was constantly manned and the building of pillboxes along the beaches of the Roseland and the Helford was virtually complete.

The Major was impressed with this veteran of the first war who had also seen service in India and the two promised to keep in touch. The Port Security Policeman had offered to give the Major a tour of the harbour by boat and the chance to see a little more of what his role entailed and they had settled on Monday as a suitable day. The Major was keen to establish just how vulnerable Falmouth was to a commando style raid.

Churchill was concerned over the use of the Schnellboot as a fast raider. There was some evidence the German Navy had used them to lay mines in the shipping lanes off the south Cornish coast. They had agreed to meet in the Seamen's Bethel at ten o'clock. The Major had explained he was staying with his parents over the weekend and to get in touch with him there should arrangements need to be changed. With a shake of the hand, they had parted and the Major had walked up Quay Street to go and rescue Elizabeth before she was tempted to spend too much money.

As the Major drove down the hill, past the Swan pool and up towards Golden Bank, the sun had come out from behind the cloud and bathed the Cornish countryside in glorious spring sunshine. They smiled at each other but didn't say a lot during the drive through the narrow and winding lanes to Bosvarren House. Their thoughts were focused on their first weekend together.

The Major turned left at the crossroads and they headed through the hamlet of Lamanva. When they reached the ornate gateposts by the lodge of Bosavick House the Major tuned left between two ivy covered granite gateposts up a narrow treelined lane. Elizabeth felt her mouth go dry as the nerves began to play.

"I do hope your parents like me, Zac," she said looking at the Major for assurance.

"You have nothing to worry about," he said kindly. "Mother was absolutely delighted when I told her I was bringing you."

“But that could be just because she doesn’t get to see her son very much,” Elizabeth countered. The Major raised an eyebrow.

“Once she’s given me a kiss and a hug, she will forget I am there. She will be glad of some female company. Remember she had two sons, so I am sure you will hit it off,” said the Major as he turned right off the lane into a short drive.

“Here we are. Built about the time of the Battle of Waterloo, although the settlement here goes right back into the Middle Ages,” said the Major as he turned off the engine.

“It looks very grand,” said Elizabeth peering through the trees and shrubs at the roof and chimneys.

“Let’s go and make the introductions first,” said the Major taking Elizabeth by the hand. “I’ll come back and get your case in a minute.” He led Elizabeth round the corner of the house to the front where she got her first full glimpse of this impressive house. There were three storeys and a small wing off on the side they had parked the car.

“It used to be a rectory,” said the Major.

“It’s much bigger than our little farmhouse outside Padstow,” said Elizabeth gazing up at the five windows than ran across the front of the house. “And what a lot of garden,” she added looking around at the vast lawn that seemed to disappear off in several directions behind various beds of flowering shrubs and trees with a carpet of bluebells beneath.

"It's just under an acre," said the Major remembering how he and his brother had loved the freedom to roam and play as they were growing up. He led Elizabeth up the granite steps that led to the front door as the ground level was half way up the first storey. Elizabeth presumed the basement level had been the servants quarters originally. Then a thought struck her with terror. 'Did they still have servants?' The Major had never spoken of them, though one of his letters had referred to a nanny when he and his brother were young. Elizabeth wondered if it was all going to be a little too grand for Miss Treluckey as the nerves got the better of her. She didn't have time to dwell on her thoughts for as they reached the top step the door was swung open and a grey haired man in his early sixties stood there with a beaming smile. Elizabeth found herself brushing down her ATS uniform as if she was about to go on parade.

"Father," said the Major throwing his arms around his parent.

"It's good to see you, my boy," he replied and then pushing his son to one side turned to Elizabeth and said,

"And you must be the beautiful Miss Elizabeth." Elizabeth felt herself blushing as she held out her hand to shake Mr Trevennel's hand. "Isaac has told us very little about you, which must mean he's serious about you, so it's good to finally meet you."

"Father don't embarrass the lady before we've got inside," said the Major with a smile.

"Oh do forgive me, I am forgetting my manners. Do come on in," Mr Trevennel said leading the way into the hallway. Elizabeth followed. It was long and thin with four mahogany doors off in all directions and the stairs that turned halfway at a window at the rear. Mr Trevennel opened a door on the right and led the new arrivals into the drawing room. This was a spacious room with two windows overlooking the front lawn. Sat in an armchair by the fireplace was Mrs Trevennel, a distinguished looking lady, about sixty, with her hair short and set in waves in a style that made her look younger than she was. She was doing some cross-stitch which she put to one side as the party entered the room.

"Isaac, dear," she said with a genuine warmth. Her son went to her and kissed her on the cheek. Elizabeth remembered Zac telling her that his mother didn't like shortened names, so she told herself to be careful to call him by his full name in conversation this weekend.

"Mother, it's good to see you," he replied. Then turning to gesture towards Elizabeth said, "May I introduce you to Miss Elizabeth Treluckey." Elizabeth stepped forward a little unsure of what manner of salutation to give but accepted the hand that was proffered and shook it lightly.

"Honoured to meet you, ma'am," Elizabeth found herself saying. Mrs Trevennel looked her up and down taking in her ATS uniform. As always, it was immaculate, although Elizabeth didn't feel confident and awaited the comment that must surely come.

"So you're the young lass that has finally tamed my Isaac after twenty nine years of my trying and failing miserably," she said with a wry smile that made Elizabeth think Zac must have inherited his humour from his mother.

"I'm not so sure I have succeeded, Mrs Trevennel," she said honestly.

"Then we must work together," the Major's mother said, "And then the poor boy won't stand a chance." Elizabeth smiled. Zac had predicted his mother would look for an ally.

"Samuel, go and tell Mrs Rickard we will have tea in fifteen minutes. Isaac and Elizabeth must be hungry after their journey. A quarter of an hour will give them time to freshen up if you show them to their rooms," said Mrs Trevennel in a manner that showed she was accustomed to organising the household.

"I need to fetch our cases in from the car first," said the Major and both father and son disappeared from the room. Elizabeth was brave enough to take a seat on the sofa.

"It's a lovely house you have, Mrs Trevennel," she ventured not quite sure what topic of conversation to strike up.

"Yes, it's a lovely spot," Isaac's mother replied wondering what sort of home Elizabeth came from. "My husband's father bought it just before the turn of the century when the rector of Constantine had to give up his country residence and just have the one vicarage in the village."

"Za...Isaac must have enjoyed growing up here," said Elizabeth hoping Zac's mother didn't notice her mistake.

“Yes I believe so. He and his brother had many happy days here. In fact, I have put you in Isaac’s old bedroom. I hope you don’t mind,” Mrs Trevennel seemed to be going out of her way to make Elizabeth feel at her ease.

“Not in the slightest,” said Elizabeth whose curiosity was aroused at the chance to see the room where her hero spent his formative years.

“Ready when you are.” It was the Major’s head that popped round the drawing room door. Elizabeth excused herself and followed him up the stairs. At the top they headed diagonally across the landing to the room at the front on the right. The Major opened the door and put Elizabeth’s case down on the floor near the bed. Elizabeth followed him in wide-eyed as she gazed around the room. There were two windows overlooking the gardens to the front of the house. The windows had shutters than folded back against the wall with window seats to be able to sit and gaze out at the views. On the side wall was a fireplace with a mantlepiece that had a clock in the middle and lines of model soldiers either side. Elizabeth could picture the young Isaac playing with them, inspiring him as to his future. There was a chest of drawers and a bookcase full of books. Elizabeth glanced quickly at the titles and they were all history books or travel books - the goldmines that had broadened the horizons of the young Trevennel mind and filled it with tales of daring-do and adventure.

“Nothing changes,” said the Major looking around at the possessions he’d treasured for years. “I hope you will be comfortable in a boy’s bedroom.”

"Well, I am in the army now," said Elizabeth picking up a lead soldier with a smile. "It will be just fine."

"We can always get Mrs Rickard to light the fire if you are cold," said the Major.

"You didn't tell me you had servants," said Elizabeth.

"We don't, not really," said the Major. "Mrs Rickard is the cook cum housekeeper. We haven't had servants since my grandparents died back in the nineteen-twenties. She comes up each day. She doesn't live in. There's been no one living in the servant's quarters since I went away to university."

"Is that the basement?" asked Elizabeth. The Major nodded. "Do we change for tea?" Elizabeth was not quite sure what the expectations would be.

"No, you're fine as you are. It will help get all the army talk out of the way at the first meal time and then we can both relax," replied the Major. He put his hands on Elizabeth's shoulders. "Have I ever told you how splendid you look in that uniform, Corporal Treluckey?" Elizabeth met his gaze and then leaned in and they kissed.

"I hope there's lots more of those this weekend," said the Major. "Come on, we'd better go down for tea," he added before Elizabeth had chance to reply and acknowledge the increased desire her heart was feeling.

Chapter Eight

Johann's muscles ached from the long day's work. He had been fetching and carrying, loading and unloading, since seven o'clock that morning. The men seemed to accept him okay. A couple of the younger Cornish lads had made fun of his accent but it was good hearted banter as they said they couldn't understand some of the phrases the older men came out with either. He had come across a couple of Irishmen and two Frenchmen in the course of his duties so he felt that he wasn't the only foreigner in the employ of Silley, Cox and Co (Engineers) Limited.

He had even got to go aboard one of the vessels wharfed at the dockside when they had to unload a consignment of boxes of small parts for the engineering workshop. He thought that might be an activity that could prove quite useful in the future.

One of the men had even pointed out the boat of the Trinity Pilot at Falmouth Mr Charles Jackson. The pilot had been awarded the M.B.E. for his heroics last July when a merchant vessel, the Marie Chandris, had been hit by a German bomb during an air raid on the docks and set on fire. Along with the assistant dockmaster Mr Jackson cut away all the mooring ropes that bound her to the wharf. He later went on board when the ship was burning fore and aft and cut away the remaining ropes that secured her to another vessel. He then made fast a tug's tow ropes to the forward bollards to allow the ship to be towed to St Mawes. On returning to the docks he then went on board the British Chancellor which was also on fire and again cut away her mooring ropes. Pilot Jackson then took a rope from this vessel onto one of the tugs to tow her out to the North Bank. He also helped release the hawsers on a third vessel, the Tiara. Falmouth was both grateful and proud.

"Does the dockyard get bombed often?" Johann asked the lad telling the story.

"Most weeks, sometimes several times a week," came the reply. The irony of the possibility of his mission being ended by a German bomb on the dockyard was not lost on Johann. He had seen the after effects of Tuesday's air raid when he arrived in Falmouth. The post office, town hall and municipal buildings on the Moor had all their windows shattered and doors and roofs blown about when a school just behind had been hit. A café nearby had also been hit resulting in three deaths. He had heard that the neighbouring town of Penryn had been worst hit that night with a number of casualties when a residential block had collapsed killing most of those who were either in the shelter or in their beds. Johann felt no sympathy. He had hoped the bombing of Britain would bring it to her knees after the planned invasion at the end of last summer was postponed. However, he did not fancy being on the receiving end of it, but that was one of the risks of employment in the dockyard.

"Johann, you can go and help those three." It was the voice of the workshop foreman calling to him. "They are going to unload some plates off the truck." Johann duly followed the other men outside and soon learned they had to lift steel plates off the truck with the help of a small crane and stand them on a rack for storage. There were twenty four in all. Two of the men stood on the truck and manoeuvred them while Johann and his colleague guided them the few yards to the rack where they were leaned upright against the standards. It was heavy, physical work even with the crane but the men worked well as a team and soon had the steel plates unloaded. It was the last activity of the day and Johann soon joined a small stream of men heading for the dockyard gates as the shift was over.

The men filed through the security shed where they were patted down to make sure they were not pilfering tools or anything else. They then had to show their papers before they were released out the other end. All seemed to go smoothly and Johann was soon passing through the gate and walking towards his lodging on Bar Road. He had found a canteen in one of the church halls that served meals to servicemen and women and other war workers. The food had been acceptable, the company accepting, and he hoped to pick up titbits of information that might prove useful to his mission. Even just keeping an eye on which units were in town made it worth the walk each evening. He was satisfied. His first week had gone well, and although he had one more shift to work on Saturday he was looking forward to getting further afield on Sunday. His appetite was growing. He decided he would have some of the canteen's new recipe, Lord Woolton Pie, which they had got from The Times newspaper last month apparently. He didn't know what the fuss amongst the canteen ladies was all about but he would enjoy this new delicacy this evening.

Chapter Nine

It was during Saturday lunch that Mrs Trevennel dropped the bombshell that was to have a deep impact on the Major. She was sat at the head of the table in the dining room with her back to the window that faced the rear garden. With the spring sunshine outside it gave her hair an almost angelic glow. They were tucking into a delicious Shepherd's Pie that Mrs Rickard had rustled up. Elizabeth didn't quite know what all the ingredients were, but the taste was sumptuous. She was singing Mrs Rickard's praises and saying she'll have to ask her for the recipe so she can send it to her mother when Mrs Trevennel said,

"We've had a letter from Geneva with some news from Vienna." Elizabeth sensed the atmosphere go electric but was unsure why, so she kept quiet.

"Geneva?" asked the Major puzzled. "Are they in Geneva?"

"No," replied his mother, "But they have got word to someone who travelled to Geneva and then wrote to us."

"Why didn't you tell me?" asked the Major with a pained expression.

"It only arrived this week," said his father countering any hint of criticism that may have been concealed in the Major's question. "And to be totally honest," he continued, "Your mother and I don't quite understand all that it says."

“May I see it,” asked the Major as he scooped another forkful of potato into his mouth.

“Excuse me,” said his father as he rose from the table to collect the letter from the study.

“The news is probably three or four months out of date,” said his mother wanting to manage the expectations her younger son might have of her revelation.

“But it’s much more recent than the letter from February thirty-nine,” said the Major. “That in itself has to be good.” He wondered just what this letter might contain. “Who is it from?” he asked.

“Some American chap at the agency who had been in Vienna over the New Year period and then wrote when he got to Geneva,” said Mrs Trevennel.

“Perhaps he felt it was not safe to write from Vienna,” mused the Major as his father returned and handed him a small handwritten envelope addressed to Mr & Mrs Trevennel. The Major quickly pulled a single sheet of paper from inside. He read it out loud.

“Geneva, January 14th 1941. Dear Mr and Mrs Trevennel, Please excuse a stranger writing to you but I was recently in Vienna for the New Year’s Concert and had the privilege of meeting your son on a couple of occasions. On the last of those he asked if I could get word to you as he felt it was not safe for him to do so. These are the messages he urged me to include. I think I have remembered them all as he said them.

"February 1939. Spent three months as guest of F then home.... Chaplain at Christ Church baptised J to Joanne & M to Michael... J & M Josh 2.6. ... G Dan 6. 4. me.

"I hope they mean something to you. Joseph looked thin and worried but otherwise seemed in good health. I am shortly to return to the USA so do not return to Vienna.

"Yours sincerely, Richard Peters. UP."

The Major looked up, looked at both his parents in turn and then said,

"So Joseph was alive and well at the beginning of this year. That is most heartening news."

"It is, I agree," said his father. "But we can't figure out what all the initials mean. Is it some kind of code? Do you recognise anything? You and he were always making up codes when you were boys, sending messages to each other that your mother and I had no idea what you were saying." Mr Trevennel looked at his son hoping for some glimmer of a breakthrough.

"No, there's nothing here like any of our codes," said the Major after a moment's pause while he ran some of his boyhood inventions through his mind and tested them against what was written.

"This 'Spent three months as a guest of F then home,'" said Mr Trevennel quoting the letter from memory showing how over the last few days he and his wife had spent hours agonising over what it could possibly all mean. "Who is F? Did he have any friends or colleagues whose name began with F?"

"Frederick? Frank? Francis? Finley? Farrington?" chimed in Mrs Trevennel rehearsing the conversation she'd had with her husband. "Fritz?" she concluded with a shrug of the shoulders.

"Wait a minute," said the Major reaching into his breast pocket and pulling out his own letter from his brother that Elizabeth had seen him read last summer. He scanned the page. "In this letter he calls Hitler the Fuhrer the first time he mentions him, then simply shortens it to F. So F is Fuhrer. He's saying he was a guest of Hitler for three months. In other words he was arrested and imprisoned."

"Oh my poor boy," said Mrs Trevennel with a look of anguish on her face.

"But he was then released as he says, 'Then home'," said the Major reassuringly.

"So what's all this baptised at Christ Church part? Has he renounced his Jewish upbringing?" asked Mrs Trevennel with a deep concern in her voice.

"He only says J and M. I don't think he mentions himself. It may be a way of protecting Jemimah and Malachi." The Major broke off to explain to Elizabeth. "Jemimah is my brother's Austrian wife. Malachi is their son. Joseph has joint British and Austrian citizenship but Jemimah and Malachi are just Austrian. Obviously all three of them are Jews." Elizabeth nodded her appreciation as the Major turned back to his parents.

"They have been given Christian names. Joanne and Michael. It's so they won't stand out as Jews to the Nazis," said the Major.

“Are they ashamed of being Jews? Why wouldn’t they want to stand out? Are they not proud of who they are?” asked Mrs Trevennel not understanding the import of what her son was trying to tell her.

“It could be a matter of life and death,” the Major said bluntly. “Joseph is trying to protect his wife and child. Christ Church is the British Embassy chapel. It’s in central Vienna, just off the Rennweg. The chaplain is providing them with some documentation they can use to say they are not Jews. It may save them from undue attention from the Nazis. It used to have a British chaplain but he got recalled in September 1938, so goodness knows who’s officiating there now. But they seem to be helpful.”

“I assume the church has links with our intelligence services for you to know all that,” said Mr Trevennel quietly. The Major just shrugged his shoulders unwilling to confirm his father’s suspicions.

“I don’t get the next bit. The Josh 2.6. obviously applies to Jemimah and Malachi and the G Dan 6.4. to Joseph, but what does it mean?” asked the Major.

“We’ve puzzled over that for hours, dear,” said his mother with a tinge of sadness in her voice.

“That’s why we’d hoped you might recognise one of your codes?” said his father feeling equally helpless. “If J and M are Jemimah and Michael, who is G?”

“Perhaps it’s the chaplain,” said the Major without conviction.

"May I see the letter," asked Elizabeth taking everyone by surprise.

"Sure," said the Major handing over the thin piece of paper. Elizabeth studied it for a moment and then said,

"They're Bible references. I'm sure. Excuse me, I'll fetch mine." She rose from the table where all thought of progressing onto dessert had vanished. The Trevennels looked at each other in silence not quite knowing what it was Elizabeth had latched onto. She returned a few moments later with a black leather bound book.

"Joshua two six," she said to herself as she leafed through the gilt edged pages. Finding what she wanted she read,

"She had brought them up to the roof of the house, and hid them with the stalks of flax, which she had laid in order upon the roof." Everyone just looked at her bemused.

"It's from the story of how Rahab hid the spies at Jericho. They are in hiding. Don't you see? Joseph is saying that Jemimah and Malachi are hiding. Possibly in a roof. In an attic perhaps." The Major's eyes lit up. He turned to his parents and exclaimed,

"Mother. Father. Elizabeth's cracked it. They are hiding. They are safe but hiding from the Nazis. That's wonderful news." His parents smiled not quite sure what to make of it all. The Major turned to the beautiful young corporal, "Elizabeth you are amazing." She blushed.

"So what's the other one?" asked Mr Trevennel.

"Daniel six four," said Elizabeth thumbing through the pages in a manner that showed she was no stranger to the contents of this book. "Then the presidents and princes sought to find occasion against Daniel concerning the kingdom; but they could find no occasion nor fault; forasmuch as he was faithful, neither was there any error or fault found in him," she read when she had found the passage. It was the Major who grasped this one.

"The authorities were looking to accuse Daniel but couldn't find anything to charge him with. If F was the Fuhrer then G must be the Gestapo. Joseph is saying they've tried to find something to charge him with but they haven't. What a relief!"

"So all three are safe and well," asked Mr Trevennel seeking confirmation that he'd understood correctly.

"Yes, father," said the Major emphatically. "They can't find any reason to re-arrest Joseph and Jemimah and Malachi are hiding somewhere."

"I would have thought being British would be reason enough to intern him, like we've done with lots of the foreign nationals here," said his father.

"Perhaps because he worked for an American press agency they've assumed he was American, not British. Though I'm sure it might have been on his Austrian papers as well if he was using those. Either way, it's a dangerous place for them all to be. I just wish I'd gone when he asked. We could have got them all out."

"You can't blame yourself for that now, son," his father said in a kindly tone. "A lot of water has gone under the bridge since then."

"I put a week's skiing over my brother and his family. If I had left the holiday and gone straight to Vienna. I am sure we could have got them out in March 1939. I'm sure we could have found a way, but when I did get there he was nowhere to be found," said the Major with deep regret and anguish in his voice.

"I think you would have been too late, even if you did go straight away," said Elizabeth. Every head turned to fix its gaze upon her. She picked up the letter and read, "'February 1939 spent three months as guest of F.' If you arrived in March he had been imprisoned for a month already." The Major picked up his letter from his brother and looked at the date: 16th February 1939.

"He must have been arrested just after sending this." The Major went quiet as the enormity of what Elizabeth had pointed out to him sank in.

"Well," said Mr Trevennel looking at his wife who had fallen strangely quiet as the conversation had progressed. "I think decoding the latest letter and knowing that when it was sent our son and his family were alive and safe, calls for a drink." He rose from the table and went over to a small mahogany drinks cabinet and pulled out a bottle. The family never did eat dessert that lunch time but the Shepherd's Pie was washed down with a glass of Dewar's White Label Scots Whiskey with toasts for the safe-keeping of the family in Vienna and to Elizabeth for being a code-breaker extraordinaire.

Chapter Ten

Johann walked past the line of buses that had brought dock workers from as far afield as Redruth, Helston and St Keverne. He was due to do the late shift, the final shift of the week as there was no working in the engineering department on a Sunday. He would start at one and work through until nine o'clock just as it was beginning to get dark. He had settled in well. The foreman seemed happy with his first few days work and his willingness to run errands and do tasks that took him to all corners of the dockyard. He had gained a reasonable grasp of the layout of the site with its four docks, the joiners' and platers' shop, the fitting shop and foundry, the timber shed and the oil basin. One of the things he was impressed by was the use of flexible pipes to refuel the vessels. The way they were used and stored would make it difficult to spot on aerial reconnaissance. Of course, there was the oil basin with its huge storage tanks but he had got the impression that there were many more that had been hidden underground in dispersed sites as there seemed to be endless pipework heading off the site. He would investigate when he had opportunity in the days ahead, but for now he was satisfied with the start he had made.

Today, however, was the beginning of starting to make his presence felt. He fished out his papers at the gate, stood nonchalantly while they were being checked and then, when they were given back to him, sauntered off to the shed where they clocked in. This would be the first opportunity to test the plan he had devised watching the process over the last couple of days.

When he reached the head of the queue and was stood before the clerk with the box of work cards, Johann said,

"Taphouse" giving the name of the fitter he had worked with yesterday. James Taphouse, a man in his forties, had told him yesterday he wasn't working this weekend as he was going to Camborne for his cousin's wedding. Johann decided he would try clocking in as Taphouse so his presence in the dockyard that day would not show up in the records. As long as none of the fitter's colleagues didn't see or hear him do it, he was certain he would get away with it. Taphouse was unlikely to know until he picked up his wage packet at the end of the next week, and would he really return a bit of extra cash or stay quiet and pocket it thinking the wages' clerk must have made a mistake. Even if he questioned it the records would say the clerk's amount was correct.

The clerk in front of him thumbed through the work cards and pulled out the one for Taphouse, James R. and handed it over to Johann. He went across the room and dropped it in the vast rack of slots in the wooden board that was designed to carry the cards of every man in the dockyard at any given time. During the shift a clerk would make an entry on the card recording the presence, the card would be used in reverse for signing out and then the card at the end of the week would be used by the wages' clerk to calculate the pay to be received. The fact that Taphouse, like most of the men in the dockyard, worked the Saturday shift most weekends, meant he was less likely to spot the financial irregularity in his favour. Johann left the shed and walked across to the Platers' Shop feeling rather pleased with himself. He was so engaged in his own plans for mischief that the dockyard train had to whistle at him to step aside of the rails as they passed the head of No 3 dock, the dry dock. This was going to be a good day.

A sombre mood settled over Bosvarren House during the Saturday afternoon after the contents of Joseph's letter had been deciphered. The enormity of the situation of having loved ones hiding from the authorities in Vienna who were obviously looking for opportunity to incarcerate them was percolating the consciousness. The Major knew full well that the intelligence reports emanating from occupied Europe did not bode well. Only on Thursday had he been informed that the French Police in Paris had arrested about one thousand foreign Jews and handed them over to the Germans who were now in the process of deporting them. The Major knew he could never divulge to his parents the secret intelligence he was party to or the means by which the UK government were made aware of it. He also knew that if he could share it with them it would not ease their burden for their oldest son, his wife and child.

It was about three o'clock Elizabeth, who had been sat on her bed reading having wisely made herself scarce, became conscious of someone sobbing. She tiptoed out onto the landing and realised it was coming from the drawing room downstairs. Wondering whether it was her place to investigate further, she made her way downstairs and was at the halfway turn when she heard footsteps across the hallway. She stepped back to stay out of sight and remained to see what would happen.

It was obvious by now it was Mrs Trevennel who was sobbing and both the Major and his father had gone into the drawing room. The door had been left ajar and Elizabeth was able to hear all that took place. Mrs Trevennel was clearly upset by the fact that her family had been baptised into the Christian church. Perhaps, it was the one target she could find to vent her feelings, or perhaps, although she and her husband had not practised their faith with the devotion and commitment of the previous generation, it was still ingrained within the thinking and the emotions. She kept asking,

"What will become of them?" and both her husband and the Major tried to reassure her but without giving false hope that all would end well, their efforts seemed to make little impact.

"What am I left with?" she wailed. "A letter."

"We should be grateful for that," said her husband. "I am sure there are many families that don't even have that to ease their concerns," he continued looking at his son for support.

"Yes, yes," said the Major. "I am sure there are many families who are worse off than we are." He was certain the platitude was of no comfort whatsoever. It distressed him to see his mother so upset, especially as he carried a burden of guilt for not having done what he could to help immediately when his brother had written to him back in February 1939.

"What am I left with?" Mrs Trevennel repeated the question. "Christ Church. Joanna and Michael. A place and a name is all I have."

"Then cling to what you have, treasure it, and we will see what tomorrow brings," said Mr Trevennel.

"I fear it's more than many will have, mother," said the Major. "This war is a dastardly business and the sooner Hitler and his henchmen are defeated the better it will be for all the world." Elizabeth felt she was intruding on the family's sorrow and quietly made her way back to the bedroom and closed the door.

It was about half an hour later Elizabeth felt brave enough to venture downstairs. She poked her head round the drawing room door. Mrs Trevennel was sat with her back to the door. Mr Trevennel was sat in an armchair and noticed her appearance.

"You'll find Isaac in the garden, my dear," he said kindly. "Down by the lazy tree." Elizabeth thanked him and headed out the front door, down the steps and onto the lawn. She was unsure which direction to head in but as Mr Trevennel had said 'down' she'd follow the slope. Elizabeth wondered what kind of tree a lazy tree was. She wandered past an old oak, a couple of firs and an ash tree and that virtually exhausted her knowledge of dendrology. She spotted a Cornish hedge with a small gateway. She went through it and as the vista opened out again she saw the lazy tree. She recognised it instantly, not because of its leaves but because one of its branches had stooped low to form a chair in which one could lay and let the world go by. Occupying its embrace was the Major. He looked up as Elizabeth approached and smiled. He moved his legs to allow her to sit beside him and took her hand.

“Zac, how are you doing?” she asked gently stroking his cheek.

“I’m doing okay,” he said smiling weakly. “Today’s news is far better than any I have had for two years, but the situation is serious, even desperate and one can’t help feeling so inadequate. If only there was something I could do.”

“But you are already doing it,” said Elizabeth reassuringly. “You are doing your utmost to help defeat Hitler and the Nazis and that will be the best way you can help at this time. In the future, who knows, there may be something specific you can do for Joseph and his family. But if it was me hiding in an attic then I’d like to think my family were doing all they could to defeat the evil that had put me there. So knowing that Britain and her Empire are standing alone against Hitler and knowing that their brother and uncle is part of the British army doing that will provide them with hope.”

“I do hope so,” said the Major. “But not knowing is so hard, and especially hard on mother. She really broke down and cried earlier.” Elizabeth squeezed his hand as she could feel his pain. “I am so glad we are here this weekend,” the Major continued. “It was good for me to be here to help reassure her, and it’s good for me that you are here with me.” He squeezed Elizabeth’s hand in return. She smiled as he continued,

“We certainly would not have fathomed out what Joseph’s letter meant without you. You are a star. Thank you. I am so grateful. I haven’t read the Mikra in ages.”

“Mikra?” Elizabeth asked.

“The Hebrew Scriptures,” replied the Major. “Not that I could have read Daniel. Much of what the prophet has written is in Aramaic and I wouldn’t have a clue. So it was good you were able to come to our family’s aid. Thank you.” The Major jumped up and stood up, turned to Elizabeth, took both her hands and put them on his shoulders and stepped in and held her in his arms and kissed her intently on the lips. Elizabeth returned the passion and felt the desire rise within her. Her hands slid down the Major’s back and she pulled him in close kissing him all the while.

“You are beautiful,” breathed the Major, his hands running up over her shoulders and brushing her hair back from her face. His hands slid back across her checks and held her neck, allowing his thumbs to caress her earlobes. Elizabeth sighed with desire. She had never felt like this before, her whole body tingling. They continued kissing for several minutes until breathless they stopped gazing into each other’s eyes with an intensity only known by those in love.

It dawned on Elizabeth today was the first time she had seen the Major out of his uniform and he cut a dashing figure in his white shirt and slacks. He admired her in her yellow summer dress with the sweetheart neckline. The dress showed off her figure to full advantage dropping to just above the knee.

“I say,” said the Major breaking the moment. “Do you fancy going to the picture house this evening? It will do us good after this afternoon.”

“What films are showing?” asked Elizabeth.

"I haven't the faintest idea," replied the Major. "I'm sure mother and father will have the Packet which will have an advertisement that will tell us." He looked at his watch. "We'd better go up to the house for tea and I'll ask for the paper."

Whilst waiting for Mrs Rickard to set the table for tea, Elizabeth and Isaac poured over the Falmouth Packet. There were three cinemas to choose from: St George's, the Grand and the Odeon.

"What about Will Hay in the Ghost of St Michael's at the Grand?" asked Elizabeth.

"Isn't that about a school that goes to the Isle of Skye?" asked the Major. "Not my first choice," he said honestly. "What about the Ghost Train at the Odeon?" he suggested.

"That's the remake of the Arnold Ridley play," said Elizabeth. "It stars Arthur Askey. I like him. Sounds good to me."

"The story is set in Cornwall and I believe they filmed some of it down here too," said the Major.

"That settles it," said Elizabeth. "As long as you don't spend the whole film playing spot the location!" And with that tea was ready.

Chapter Eleven

After tea Elizabeth went up and changed into the one evening dress she had brought with her for the weekend. It was a long dark blue dress, slender in line with a square neck and sleeves that finished just above the elbow. Elizabeth put on her favourite white cardigan over the top and took a pair of white gloves. She felt she was fit for a ball although the Odeon Picture House was their destination. The Major would be in his uniform, which would guarantee them entry even if the sign said 'Full House', and she wanted to look the part as the blonde beauty on his arm. With a final brush of the hair which she wore down, she headed across the landing to the stairs.

Feeling like a Hollywood starlet as her dress swished over her legs, she slowly and with deliberate and careful footing descended the stairs. She had just reached the bottom stair when she became aware of the conversation in the drawing room.

"So mother what do you make of Elizabeth?" the Major was asking. Elizabeth paused waiting to hear the reply. She almost wished she hadn't.

"She's very pretty, my dear, but she's not one of us," Mrs Trevennel told her son.

"Mother," said Isaac half in indignation, half in question.

"Is she going to become a righteous proselyte or are you going to marry a goy?" she asked fiercely. The Major didn't answer. “Don’t tell me you are going like your brother and going off the derech as well?”

“I will always respect my upbringing. It is part of who I am. But you and father have hardly been defenders of the faith. When was the last time you attended the synagogue? And at lunch it was Elizabeth who knew her way round the Mikra, not any of us.” The Major knew his grandparents had been devout members of the community in Penzance, but his parents had been lax in their observance of the customs and rituals for most of his lifetime. They had just lived a more secular lifestyle, and so the Major had been a little taken aback by his mother’s reaction to her sons’ dealings whether in Vienna or here now.

“There are never enough here in Falmouth to even read the scrolls,” said Mrs Trevennel referring to a Jewish law that required ten adult men to be present before the ancient Scriptures could be read. “Going to the nearest synagogue in Plymouth or in Devonport is just out of the question. The rabbis say we should not walk more than half a mile on the Sabbath. But that doesn’t mean my son has to take up with a goy. Even your older brother married a good Jewish girl.”

“Mother, I am particularly fond of Elizabeth,” the Major stated. Elizabeth didn’t know whether to be hurt or happy. Hurt that after this afternoon’s passionate embrace, he could only describe his feelings as fondness. Happy that she was hearing him for the first time publicly declare that he had feelings for her. The Major continued, “She is beautiful, sincere, kind, clever, and a devout Christian believer and, good grief, is that the time? We must get going if we are to make our film in Falmouth. We’ll talk further on this matter.”

Blushing with embarrassment at Isaac's wholesome description of her, she decided it was time to make her presence downstairs known and she stepped onto the tiled hallway and towards the drawing room, meeting the Major as he was coming out.

"I was just about to call you," he said. "We need to get going. Just stick your head in here to say cheerio to mother." Elizabeth wasn't sure she wanted to confront her detractor so soon after hearing the Major's mother's true feelings about her, but she complied with Isaac's wishes and nodded a farewell.

Elizabeth was in two minds as they drove the short distance into Falmouth. Should she reveal to Isaac that she had heard his conversation with his mother, or would he be upset at the thought of her eaves-dropping on his private conversations? She decided she would say nothing as she did not want it to spoil a rare and wonderful evening out together.

The Major parked on the Moor and they walked the short distance down Killigrew Street past the bombed out Methodist Church undergoing repair and across the road to the cream tiled cinema building. The neon sign that had shone so brightly before the war was gone, a casualty of when the church across the road suffered a direct hit last October killing four soldiers from the Worcestershire Regiment and Pioneer Corps and two teenage boys from the church. The four large first floor windows of the cinema had been replaced but were covered inside with thick black-out material stuck to the glass to prevent them shattering and falling on anyone below. The Major bought their tickets and they made their way into the vast auditorium. They were sat in the front row of the Circle so the heads of those in front in the seven hundred seats in the stalls would not get in the way.

The newsreel showed pictures from the Blitz on London with firefighters tackling burning buildings. The announcer reported that Home Secretary Herbert Morrison had nationalised the country's fire services. There was a quick glimpse of the damaged aircraft that brought Rudolf Hess, Hitler's deputy, down in Scotland. It finished with shots of the 60,000 crowd at Wembley Stadium watching the Cup Final which saw Preston North End and Arsenal draw one-all.

Elizabeth thoroughly enjoyed the Ghost Train. She jumped when Price's car crashed off the road but was delighted when the Major put his arm round her and pulled her close. Her head lingered on his chest as the lights came up. She wondered if there really were Fifth Columnists in Cornwall smuggling arms on the railway. She would certainly keep her eyes peeled next time she took the train home from Bodmin to Padstow for a weekend leave.

"Well, I'm glad nothing really exciting's happened," said the Major as they got back into the car. It was a slow drive back through the winding lanes with the grills dimming the headlights until they were of little use at all. Elizabeth was grateful when the Major turned into the drive of Bosvarren House. The place was in darkness and it reminded Elizabeth of the farm at home where she had become accustomed to moving about in the pitch black. The Major used his torch to guide them up the steps to the front door and they let themselves in. Pulling the black out curtain back across the door, the Major then reached and turned on the light. It was just gone ten o'clock but the

Major's parents had retired for the night and the young couple were left to their own devices.

"Fancy a Horlicks? Or I expect I can do you a hot Bovril if you would like one?" asked the Major as he led Elizabeth towards the kitchen. "I'll have a Horlicks, please Zac. We've not been to the football," she replied and followed him into Mrs Rickard's domain. The Major was soon warming some milk on the stove while Elizabeth sat in a highbacked chair, the only seat in the room which was obviously the cook's throne. The Major was rummaging around for something to eat and unearthed some carrot cake in a tin and cut them both a slice.

"Quite domesticated," teased Elizabeth.

"Oh I am a dab hand at finding a snack once cook has gone home," said the Major with a grin that recalled nights when he and his brother had raided the kitchen long after their parents had gone to sleep.

The couple enjoyed their drink and Mrs Rickard's carrot cake as they chatted about the film. The Major, leaning against the solid oak kitchen table, said that he thought he had spotted Liskeard Station in the film, otherwise the only other location he recognised was the railway as it passed Langstone Rock near Dawlish.

"That was where Arthur Askey pulled the communication chord to make the train stop so he could get his hat," said the Major.

"So you were playing spot the location!" exclaimed Elizabeth in mock horror. "Take a beautiful girl to the pictures and all you're interested in is where the film was shot." The Major put his mug down and went across and kissed Elizabeth.

"Will that get me out of jail, or do I still have to pass 'Go!'?" he asked referring to the game that had become all the rage just before the war.

"I could not stay angry with you for long if you are willing to make things up to me like that," said Elizabeth smiling as she yawned. "It's been an eventful day, so I think I should retire. Thank you for a lovely evening, Zac."

"Goodnight sweetheart," he said. "I'm just going to rinse through the evidence of our late night feasting, and then I shall hit the sack too." Elizabeth gave him a peck on the cheek as she swished past and headed for the stairs. The Major stood watching her go. He admired everything about her. Her beautiful long blonde hair, her warm friendly face with a ready smile, her sparkling blue eyes that showed a soul that was really alive, her slender figure, and long legs. The Major remembered how it was her eyes that had first grasped his attention the first evening he met her and she had fallen off the stile into his arms as they walked across the fields back to her parents' farm. He had met a lot of beautiful girls but none had captured his heart in the way that Elizabeth had succeeded in doing. She was beautiful on the inside too. Kind, truthful, loving, considerate, hard-working, loyal, intelligent. He felt she was perfect. If only his mother would see that as well. He finished his drink and put the dishes into the large Belfast sink and ran some water over them. His mind was not on the job and they were not entirely clean as he stood them on the draining board to drip dry overnight.

Elizabeth had cleaned her teeth, brushed her hair and changed from her blue dress into her cream satin nightdress with its ivory lace trim. She was sat on the bed, having turned off the ceiling light and was checking her nails by the light on the beside table when she heard the door handle turn. She looked up to see the Major slip quietly into her room and shut the door behind him. She was shocked. He hadn't even knocked. She didn't know whether to throw him out immediately or wait to see just what he wanted. Curiosity got the better of her so she said nothing as he walked round the bed and came and sat next to her.

"I couldn't let this wonderful evening end without saying goodnight to you properly," he said in a low voice so the conversation wouldn't carry across the landing in case his parents were still awake. Elizabeth wondered just what this goodnight would entail. Her bed jacket was hanging on the back of the door and she felt very undressed for this encounter. The Major with his index finger lifted her hair which was hanging down in front of her and gently brushed it back behind her shoulder exposing a little more of her smooth silky skin. On his way back his finger ran slowly over the ivory lace of the shoulder strap and just as she wondered where it would stop, he pulled her in and kissed her. Once she was over the initial shock, Elizabeth responded to his affection and put her arms round his back and pulled him close. The kiss was passionate and the intensity rose. The Major's hands held Elizabeth's shoulders and he caressed them gently. He then ran his hands across her back and as she arched his mouth planted little kisses along her neck until he nibbled on her ear. She sighed as his lips moved back onto hers and they kissed again. His hands moved back onto the wide straps covering her shoulder blades and there the left hand stayed while the right ran up and over her shoulder and down the lace until it cupped her breast and his fingers closed about it. Elizabeth felt her flesh engorge as his hand caressed her bosom and her head was spinning. Her body tingled with desire for this handsome man but her heart knew this wasn't right.

Suddenly the Major stood up and began to take off his tunic. Elizabeth sensed he was aroused and knew she had to act fast.

"Zac, no," she said. "Not now." The Major froze poleaxed. He couldn't believe his ears. He had felt her body respond to his touch and felt the physical contact was an extension of his expression of love.

"It's not that I don't want you, Zac. I do. I love you," she said her head racing for the right words to say.

"Then what?" he asked perplexed by the sudden application of the brakes.

"I want to give myself wholly to you and please you in every way, but the right place to do that is in marriage, and so we must wait until then, please Zac," she explained desperately hoping that she didn't sound too forward and hadn't ruined any prospects of the Major asking for her hand one day.

"I see," said the Major with the clarity of a moorland pony engulfed in some Cornish mizzle. He sat back down again. "I'm sorry," he said taking Elizabeth's hand. "I didn't mean to upset you."

“I am not upset,” said Elizabeth. “I am thrilled that you desire me and please know that I want you too. I really do. But I also believe that God intends these pleasures for a man and wife and that’s not what we are. Maybe one day you’ll ask me,” she said with a look that said, ‘Don’t even think about asking now!’ “And I’ll be delighted. What we have in our friendship is special. Let’s not spoil it by rushing things.”

Now it was Zac’s turn for his head to spin. He was confident he had read the signs correctly. He had behaved as any full-blooded male would have done with a beautiful young woman who had kissed him so passionately pressing the delightful form of her body into his. Yet what had he done wrong? Why this sudden rejection? He even wondered if his mother’s attitude towards Elizabeth had anything to do with it. Perhaps his mother had said to her what she had said to him. The Bible on her bedside table suddenly caught his attention. He leaned across and picked it up.

“Is this really the book you live by?” he asked wondering whether even this was the cause of the impasse.

“I try to,” said Elizabeth. “With God’s help.”

“Why?” the Major asked. He had never come across anyone like this before and while he found Elizabeth attractive in every way, he was now feeling frustrated.

“I guess it’s the Maker’s instruction manual. Things usually work better when you follow the Maker’s guidelines,” said Elizabeth gently. “I’ve seen people wreck others’ lives as well as their own when they don’t follow what God wants.”

"And that's why...." The Major's voice trailed off as the realisation began to dawn on him that Elizabeth was staying true to her convictions. He began to admire her in a new way for he realised that took strength and depth of character. "Would I have to convert from Judaism if we were ever to...?" he asked struggling for the right word to complete the sentence knowing he didn't want his question to sound like a feeble attempt at a marriage proposal.

"Nobody is going to make you do anything. True conversion does not commit men against their will. It's between you and Almighty God," said Elizabeth respectfully. "My faith does not renounce Judaism, it fulfils it. The church is the branch grafted into the vine. The Jews are still God's chosen people." She paused as he drank in what she was saying. She added, "I am sure that's why Hitler hates them so much. He rejects the God of the Bible and so he rejects God's people."

"Too many people have rejected the Jews over the centuries," said the Major. "Our history seems to be one of persecution."

"There were times when you saw God's favour," said Elizabeth. "David was a victorious king, and Solomon, had a wealth and a wisdom that the world came to see. And God will favour your people once again. The words of the prophets will come true."

"Now you sound like a Zionist," said the Major.

"No, I see that as a political movement," said Elizabeth with a grasp of world affairs that few women her age could replicate.

“I just believe that when God says something He will bring it to pass, like He did in the coming of Messiah.”

“But how can one who failed to re-establish the kingdom in Jerusalem be Messiah?” asked the Major. “Christians make such claims about the incarnation and the deity of Jesus that cannot possibly be true.” Elizabeth thought for a minute before answering.

“Who is Isaiah describing when he talks of the suffering servant? It’s of a person, not a nation.” answered Elizabeth, grateful for the studies and discussions she had sat in with her parents at the Gospel Hall in Padstow. “Messiah had to suffer before He comes in power and glory. The Old Testament Scriptures contain more than three hundred references to the coming of the Messiah written at least four hundred years before the birth of Jesus. Yet He fulfilled them all. Don’t take my word for it. Read it for yourself. Read the eye witness accounts of his life and decide for yourself. But not right now, Zac. It’s getting late and we should get some sleep.”

“On that we can agree,” said Zac with a smile. He stood up, took her hand and kissed it. “You never cease to amaze me,” he said as he walked round the bed. “Sleep well. I’ll see you in the morning.” He closed the door quietly behind him and was gone.

Chapter Twelve

The hammering on the door was getting more and more intense as Johann roused himself from his deep slumber. He pulled back the covers, looked at the clock to see it was five to one and waddled towards the door. He opened it and to his surprise stood there with a candle on the landing was Mrs Browning. Her hair was under a hair net and she wore an overcoat over her thick woollen pyjamas.

"Mr Johann, "she said urgently. "The air raid siren is going. Are you going to come with us down to the shelter? Get a coat on, if you do, as it can be quiet chilly. I told Mr Greensill, the warden for our street, that you would be, so get a move on." Her comments had moved rapidly from question to command and Johann was left with no option but to grab a coat and to follow her down the stairs, out through the kitchen where she blew out the candle, outside and down the garden path to where her husband had half buried the Anderson shelter.

Jones, who lodged in the room across the landing from Johann, obviously familiar with the routine given the number of air raids Falmouth had suffered, was already sat in one of the two deckchairs that were placed on the earthen floor. Johann guessed rightly that the other seat, a small upright armchair was for Mrs Browning, so he settled into the wood and canvas contraption that he felt wouldn't offer him much sleep.

Mrs Browning came in, adjusted the canvas sacking that sufficed for the door and then relit her candle and placed it carefully in a large flower pot in the middle before easing back into her armchair. The siren had ceased its merciless wail and the occupants of the dank and dusty shelter sat watching the dancing shadows from candle flame. When after ten minutes it was obvious there was to be no immediate deluge of German bombs the conversation started. Johann was rather guarded, not wanting to give too much away, but he needn't have worried as the other two were glad to have a new audience with which to regale their tales.

Johann found that Mr Browning worked on the railways as a guard and often did nights on trains going up to London, a matter which had caused his wife some concern with all the bombing going on. Only once had his train been caught and that was on the single line through Falmouth when earlier this year in January bombs landed nearby in some allotments and cut a fuel pipeline. His train was derailed in the cutting between Pennance Road bridge and Swanvale but Mr Browning was unscathed. The two passengers on his Sunday evening train were shaken and scratched but otherwise unhurt. The driver and firemen survived intact. Three bombs had hit Whitethorn Farm and also damaged the Shell Mex pipeline but fortunately the fuel did not ignite. One air raid warden had a lucky escape when one of the bombs landed in an allotment producing a crater fifty feet by twenty five feet and the debris rained down on him as he lay flat in the road. His helmet showed a hefty dent so it had obviously saved him from serious injury.

"So," said Mrs Browning finishing her story, "There I was all worried about him up London and his train gets hit just a half mile from 'ome!"

Jones, who apparently also worked on the railways in the goods yard, spoke of the parachute mine dropped in the inner harbour in a raid towards the end of February that went off almost a fortnight later when a team of divers were trying to deal with it. The diver's body was never found. His five colleagues on the dive barge were all killed and those on the mouse were injured with one succumbing to his injuries a short while later.

"Brave men," said Jones with feeling. Mrs Browning felt they needed a more cheerful subject to keep their spirits up and Johann was relieved he wasn't called on to recount any wartime experiences. Jones went on to talk of the gale back in February that had ripped nine of the town's barrage balloons from their cables. They were flying at the time. Six had come down in the neighbourhood but three had left the district altogether.

"I bet there's some farm woman who's got them for her bloomers. Good quality silk is what they say," said Mrs Browning laughing. "Not that I know," she added when the two men looked at her questioningly

Eventually the three of them decided to try and get some sleep but without much success until the all clear went at four in the morning and they were able to traipse back into the house and to their beds.

Elizabeth was dreaming of clanging bells when she finally woke and realised the telephone was ringing downstairs. As she washed in the cold water from the jug on the night stand, she heard Mrs Trevennel call out to her husband,

"Who was it this time?"

"Your sister," he replied. "Apparently they had a three hour alert in Falmouth in the small hours but it seems no bombs. So she was just ringing to check we were all ok." Elizabeth dressed and wandered down stairs into the dining room to find the Major's parents sat at either end of the table eating toast.

"Good morning," said Mrs Trevennel. "If you want some porridge I believe there is still some on the stove. Mrs Rickard doesn't come in on a Sunday morning so you'll have to help yourself. Or there's toast here on the table if you'd prefer." Elizabeth was a little taken aback. Even if Mrs Trevennel didn't regard her as daughter-in-law material she was still being civil to her guest.

Elizabeth opted for the porridge and after scooping the final bowlful from the pan sat at the table between husband and wife. Mr Trevennel spoke first.

"I'm sorry Isaac has been called into Falmouth. He had a young Home Guard messenger on his bicycle come with some message from a gentlemen Isaac saw on Friday. He said that he didn't know how long he would be but he would be back in time to get you back to Bodmin."

Elizabeth didn't know what to say. She was relieved the Major had in mind her need to be back at barracks this evening. However, the prospect of spending the day alone with his parents especially after Mrs Trevennel had revealed her thoughts to her son filled her with dread. It was Mrs Trevennel who came up with the solution.

"It's a lovely morning, dear. Why don't you take a walk in the lanes and get some spring air? Lunch will be at one."

"That sounds a lovely idea," said Elizabeth jumping at the opportunity of escape. She kindly washed up the breakfast things despite Mrs Trevennel's protests, collected her cardigan and headed out the door and up the drive. Armed with some directions from Mr Trevennel she walked up the lane towards High Cross and then descended through the twists and turns until she crossed the stream at Ponjeravah and then began the climb up into the village of Constantine. The two miles had taken her just under the hour, although she had stopped at a few gateways to examine the view, or the daisies and primroses that filled the hedgerows in places and she was in good time for the eleven o'clock service at the Wesleyan Chapel. Her cheeks were glowing from her exercise as she accepted a hymnbook and made her way into the chapel. She slid onto the end of a pew next to a couple of Land Army girls who were billeted at Treviades nearby. They were friendly and welcoming and the trio enjoyed singing the rousing opening hymn by Charles Wesley written in 1738 to celebrate his conversion "And Can It Be?" Elizabeth enjoyed the service even though it was a little different to what she was accustomed to, and then to her delight found the two girls were walking back to their farm which was halfway back to Bosvarren. The long hill out of Constantine did not seem so long or so steep with company to share the journey and friendly conversation to lighten the mood.

Feeling invigorated from her devotions and with a spring in her step Elizabeth made her way back up the drive to Bosvarren with ten minutes to spare to lunch. She was delighted to see the Major's car back outside the kitchen wing of the house. She found him talking to his parents in the drawing room. She wanted to throw her arms around his neck and kiss him but felt such a demonstrative expression of her emotions may not be appreciated by all.

It turned out the Major had been summoned by Bob Dunstan from the Port Security Police. There had been a couple of incidents in the dockyard yesterday, one resulting in the death of a man who was crushed under a pile of steel plates that had been loaded onto a rack for storage. While that appeared to be a tragic accident, the cutting of several machinery drive belts in the fitters' shop certainly wasn't and the report that a Royal Naval vessel was returning to port after it suspected its degaussing gear had been sabotaged had made Mr Dunstan wonder if even the accident was something more sinister. The two men had looked at the evidence, examined the work cards for yesterday's shift and while Mr Dunstan had spotted a couple of characters he described as agitators in the Transport and General Worker's Union, he said there was no reason to suspect them of sabotage. They had discussed what else could be done to be vigilant and agreed to consider the matter further when they met on Monday morning. The Major also brought the news that the RAF and Naval aerodromes on the north Cornish coast near Padstow had again been targeted in last night's raid. The police had reported 166 High Explosive bombs and over a thousand incendiaries had been dropped. How he accessed such information was a mystery to Elizabeth but she felt privileged he trusted her with it.

The Major was glad to be back for lunch and Mrs Rickard had certainly done them proud. It was lamb with roast potatoes, carrots, turnip and cauliflower with a gravy made from the meat juices and mint sauce made with mint picked from her cottage garden that morning. With everyone feeling a little more relaxed and cheerful, the conversation flowed. Elizabeth wondered whether Zac or his father had challenged Mrs Trevennel over her attitude as she seemed to have lost the iciness that chilled her conversation yesterday, though nothing was said that gave Elizabeth hope her opinions had changed.

Mrs Trevennel explained that they would be having two girls come for tea. They were part of the Kindertransport that had come to Britain from Austria in 1938. They were two sisters who now lived at St Joseph's in Falmouth, a large house across from the Catholic Church that used to be a convent. They were among a number looked after by Miss Davis and Miss Kitty and the Trevennels had the Jewish girls out to tea once a month.

Mr Trevennel fetched the two girls at three o'clock using his own car which Elizabeth hadn't seen as it was kept immobilised in one of the sheds of the farming hamlet that shared the drive with Bosvarren. Lieselotte was the elder, Ingrid the younger. The girls had lived in Vienna before becoming refugees and it was perhaps this connection with the city their son lived in that made the Trevennels show kindness to the girls. Realising Sunday tea with adults they didn't know was probably an ordeal for the poor girls, Elizabeth spent time chatting with Ingrid about the delightful little umbrella and handbag she had brought with her. Decorated in a pretty floral pattern it was one of the few possessions they had been able to bring out with them. After a tea of fish paste sandwiches and carrot cake, Mr Trevennel took the girls back at five thirty and the Major and Elizabeth took their leave at the same time in order to make Bodmin by seven.

Mr Trevennel had kindly said he hoped Elizabeth would visit again but there was no such offer from his wife. The Major assured his parents he would be back again while he was in Cornwall saying he wasn't due back in London until the end of the month.

The drive back to Bodmin was spent for the large part in silence. Both were assessing the weekend and didn't want to rekindle the awkward moments that had occurred. Elizabeth wondered whether her faith would be a barrier to Zac. She definitely loved him, she told herself, but would he be able to accept her especially given his mother's opposition to him marrying anyone who wasn't a Jew. She knew she was certain in her own faith so should she walk away from him? Was that the honourable thing to do even if it was the last thing she wanted to do? She felt she had done the right thing, as hard as it was, to decline his advances, but knew she would welcome them and surrender fully to them once there was a wedding ring on her finger. She was glad she had not allowed them to do anything they might regret, although she was worried she had bruised his ego in doing so. She would just wait a while and see how Zac played his hand next. If he was genuine in his love for her he wouldn't let her go.

The Major was annoyed with himself for trying to push things forward physically. He was supposed to be a gentleman but he had allowed the passion of the evening to override his judgement and he had obviously upset Elizabeth. While he admired her determination to stay true to her convictions, he was only too aware the war could snatch away the opportunity to share the passion he clearly felt for this beautiful young woman. Should he ask for her hand in marriage now and suffer the separation that their wartime service would impose upon them? That would at least give them a few snatched moments of passion together. Or should he wait and run the risk that the war could hand them a cruel twist of fate with one of them being killed? Or worse still, if he were injured? Would Elizabeth still want him then? He was also annoyed at his mother. How could she be so negative about someone as delightful as Elizabeth? His parents had been lax about their faith, only ever marking the major festivals and then usually in an understated way. His bar mitzvah was the last occasion he could recall a major celebration in the house. And that was nineteen twenty four! He knew the Talmud prohibited such a marriage but Boaz had married Ruth the Moabite widow. But had she converted first? Were her children Jewish? Would Elizabeth have to become a Jew? Would he have to become a Christian? Why was life so complicated? He needed to concentrate on his mission in Cornwall. That would give Elizabeth time to make her feelings known and he would take things from there.

It was five to seven when the Major dropped Elizabeth off at the Keep gate at the Victoria Barracks in Bodmin. It was a short but affectionate kiss as they separated with the promise to try and meet up the following weekend if duties allowed. The Major hoped the intervening week would make things clearer for them both. Elizabeth turned on her heel and walked in through the barrack gate.

Chapter Thirteen

It was a grim faced Major as he left the fourth floor of the Falmouth Hotel with Mr Dunstan on Monday morning. They had brought senior naval intelligence officers up to date with their suspicions of the weekend activity at the dockyard. The Major had also been able to use the scrambler telephone to speak directly to London. There was increased concern at the imminence of an invasion as last Wednesday a German spy was arrested in Hertfordshire shortly after parachuting in. He had dropped in on the 13th and was making his way through the lanes when a lorry driver asking for directions was suspicious at his accent, his suitcase and lack of local knowledge. The police were notified and he was soon apprehended. MI5 had broken his cover story over the weekend and the alert put out across the country for increased vigilance for other enemy agents.

The Major toured the harbour defences during the afternoon as the two men had originally planned and was pleased at what had been done with limited resources since he was in Falmouth in July 1940. The Major was still concerned about attack by fast raiding craft and said he would recommend to army chiefs the building of a six pounder battery at Middle Point below Pendennis Castle and a similar one on the St Mawes side of the river. He felt confident he could pull the strings needed to get them operational before the end of the year. The two men were also aware that the security of the port was only as strong as its weakest link and both felt that was the vast workforce. They discussed ways of vetting workers and monitoring activities in the dockyard.

The Major promised he would call back again before he left Cornwall and gave the secret serviceman details of how he could be contacted. Mr Dunstan was glad of the support as he explained that although Falmouth's ship repair facilities were among the best in the country, they often felt they were out on a limb because of their geographical position. The Major said he would try and have a word in the right ears to try and increase the security budget. He didn't tell him that he had the ear of the Prime Minister and his report on security at Cornwall's installations would precipitate increased spending by government. The Chancellor had announced back in February that the war was costing Britain £11,000,000 a day, but after the USA had passed the Lend-Lease Bill back in March the Prime Minister was hoping Parliament would support increased UK expenditure. It was with a feeling that he had done all he could for the time being that the Major drove out of the dockyard gates to spend an evening with his parents before tomorrow's visit to his next installation.

Johann had spent the day coughing and spluttering every time there was someone else within range. It was not that he was ill. He didn't even have a cold, but he needed a day off. Because of the night spent in the air raid shelter he had slept in on Sunday morning and as a consequence missed the train he wanted to catch to spy out an installation that his Abwehr masters wanted more information on. He was keen not to wait until next weekend but he was due to be in the dockyard every day until Saturday lunchtime. He didn't want to attract undue attention by just absenting himself for a day; he wanted permission to be away.

"Do you no read the posters?" said an irritated workmate who Johann made quite a show of sneezing over. "Coughs and sneezes spread diseases. Use your handkerchief, mate!" Johann didn't get his handkerchief out until he spotted the foreman come into the workshop. Then he used it to mop his brow as if he was having a hot flush. Eventually one of the other workers must have said something to the foreman as he came and told Johann to go and see the medical orderly before he infected the whole shift. Johann was a bit taken aback that the dock had its own facility. He had hoped to be told to go to a doctor's surgery in town that no one would bother checking up on. Now he had to carry off his act to convince someone with medical knowledge.

Johann sneezed all over the bald-headed orderly in his white coat as he entered his office. The man listened to Johann's chest and said there appeared to be nothing there causing any concern. He took Johann's temperature and reported that appeared perfectly normal. So Johann took his cue from the foreman and expressed his desire not to infect the rest of his shift and asked the orderly to sign him off for twenty four hours bed rest.

"You need a doctor's note for that," said the orderly. "Company policy. I'll give you a referral to Dr Lanyon but you will need to pay any doctor's fees."

Delighted Johann tucked the piece of paper in his pocket as he left the office. He was feeling better already! Just one more hour of his shift in which to keep up the pretence and then he would be free for the morrow. He would have a whole evening in which to forge the doctor's note and was sure Mrs Browning would be forthcoming with sufficient detail if he asked without arousing suspicion that he could make it seem authentic.

The sun had broken through the early cloud as the Major drove up Chapel Hill and into Fore Street on Tuesday morning. He was heading up to St Erth Hill for the inspection of his next installation. He slowed to pass a couple of Land Army girls who were leading a shire horse and wagon gently down the hill. He had just passed Esmerelda, a large house on the left, when he was brought to an abrupt stop by a Home Guard roadblock. One soldier with a rifle in his hands was stood in the road by the barrier, and at the sound of the car another was emerging from the tin hut on the verge against the hedge. The Major lowered his window and handed over his papers. The second Home Guard man did a tour of the car looking in all the windows and when he got round to his colleague asked the Major for permission to look in the boot. The Major agreed with a wry smile wondering if word had got round about the security lapse last week in Hayle. The boot was empty and the Major allowed to pass through.

He continued a short way to the brow of the hill and turned left into a field where there were two long huts, a collection of smaller ones and then behind several sets of aerials that dwarfed the little camp. He parked the car and as he was getting out was met by a man dressed in civilian clothes. He introduced himself as Mr Reardon, the person in charge of the station. The Major introduced himself and suggested he explain his business in the man's office. He took him into a wooden hut which was obviously the staff hut and canteen. At one end there was a small office and he led the Major inside. Once the door was shut, the Major explained that he was here to conduct a review of the site's security and produced the necessary authority.

The Major, who had spent the previous evening reading the 1940 Notes on the Detection Of Illicit Wireless booklet and various other papers prepared for him by the security service, asked Mr Reardon to give him a brief summary of the development of the site and a run-down of the personnel who served there. Mr Reardon explained that the General Post Office had opened the site in 1939 as part of the government's measures to discover and locate wireless traffic in the United Kingdom that was being sent for the benefit of the enemy, either by agents or persons unknown sympathetic to the Nazis. They had started with two listening positions and a direction finding capability. By October 1940 this had increased to ten positions.

The Major said it was his understanding that within a month of the war breaking out the Secret Services had dealt with all illicit wireless traffic in the UK. Mr Reardon raised an eyebrow. It was obviously new information to him. The Major continued, "I believe the Radio Security Service soon turned its attention to wireless traffic that was being created abroad by the Germans." Mr Reardon nodded. That much he had deduced.

"The operators," Mr Reardon explained, "have never been told just what it is they are listening to. It was obvious it was German Morse Code but we are unaware whose wireless traffic we are eavesdropping on." He paused, perhaps hoping some hint might be forthcoming from the Major, but there wasn't even a flicker of the eyes. “The men record the bursts of five letters onto message pads and they are then sent to an address in Barnet. Originally it was to Wormwood Scrubs but last October it changed. Occasionally we are told to send something urgently and that then gets passed on via motorcycle courier. We do have a telephone link with headquarters so they sometimes alert us to something being extra special but we are not informed and it usually passes in a day or two.”

“Your staff,” said the Major moving the conversation to safer territory, “are, I believe, a mixture of civilians and military personnel.”

“Yes,” said Mr Reardon, “We have some ex-Cable & Wireless operators, many amateurs – you know, radio hams, that were in the Voluntary Interceptors scheme that then got their call up papers – and a few that have come from the three services.”

“The blend works well?” asked the Major.

“Yes. We are very task orientated here. There is little in the way of military discipline, just the emphasis that secrecy is the key.”

“Who sets the priorities for what you listen to?” asked the Major already knowing the answer as he had sat in on one or two meetings of the fortnightly SS and SIS Committee that oversaw the day to day running of the Radio Security Service and set its priorities based on the latest intelligence.

"They are set by our Intelligence Officer Holmes who takes directions from HQ," said Mr Reardon confirming the Major's understanding of the situation.

"So how many men are posted here?" enquired the Major.

"Usually about forty," came the reply. "We have fifteen receivers in nine positions that are continuously manned by a team of seven SW1's and 27 USW's. Four SW1's are on the concentrator, one guy on maintenance and four SW1's who are specialists on the direction finding side of things. As you may be aware, we are trialling a Spaced Loop station here at St Erth." The Major nodded. "Then there's the Intelligence Officer and myself."

"You've had no security leaks as far as you are aware?" asked the Major. Mr Reardon shook his head wondering if some incident was the reason for this unannounced visit. The Major continued, "There's been no talk in the village about what goes on here, especially as I presume a number of the men are billeted in the village?"

"Yes, several live or are billeted in the village. Some travel in from Penzance. There's a bus that ferries them for their shifts. It is always on time. The men just say they are involved in 'Communications' and people accept that they can't ask questions. They realise it's part of the war effort. The Home Guard prevent anything other than ourselves or the farmer from coming on this part of the lane. Everybody else has to go round via Trenhayle or Countess Bridge Lane." Mr Reardon pulled out a small notebook from his pocket, flicked through it until he found the page he wanted and then said, "Oakes lives in the village. Griffiths married in November last year so he and his wife are in the village. Hanlon has a Scots wife. She teaches English at Hayle Grammar School."

"I bet that confuses the Cornish," smiled the Major injecting a note of lightness into proceedings. Reardon ignored the remark.

"We've been here almost two years so I think the community now accept us and to my knowledge there's been nothing that causes concern. As you'll see, some of the men are in Home Guard uniform, some wear the uniform of the Royal Observer Corps and others, especially the GPO guys, are in civvies."

"Are you aware that the Radio Security Service has been transferred from the War Office?" asked the Major.

"Yes, I have received official notification," replied Mr Reardon. "All I know is that the base will be militarised either later this year or early next year. I've not told the men."

"As I understand it, that will put all your men, should they choose to stay, into the uniform of the Royal Signals. But that allows the line of 'Communications' to still be used as an adequate explanation." Again this was new to Mr Reardon and he wondered just how well that would go down with some of the older GPO men.

"Perhaps you'd like to show me around," said the Major. It was more of an order than a request but Mr Reardon was only too relieved to move attention from him to the operations they were conducting. The two men got up and went out into the larger part of the hut.

“This is the room where the man can come when they are off duty. They eat their sandwiches here and as you can see we have an urn for them to make a brew.”

“You have water laid on here?” asked the Major.

“We do now. We didn’t at first. We’ve had to sink a borehole down one hundred and ten feet to get water which is now pumped up to a tank in the corner of the field. Caused a bit of a stir with some of the houses just down the lane. Apparently we lowered the water table and they were unable to get any water from their wells. So we’ve run a pipe across the fields to supply them and they’re happy enough with the arrangement.”

“But you’ve no cooking facilities? No cook?” asked the Major showing his concern for men who were spending long hours on duty for their country.

“No,” said Mr Reardon rather sheepishly. The Major turned towards the door and Mr Reardon took the cue. He led them out into the field and to the left where set at a ninety degree angle to the hut they’d just left was a similar hut of wooden construction but with its windows blackened out. The door was at the southern end and they entered a large room lit by electric lamps on the ceiling with two banks of HRO radios on a long desk either side. There was a table in the middle and sat on hard back wooden chairs were operators with headphones on. No one seemed to notice their arrival and the Major stood just surveying the scene for a moment before Mr Reardon spoke.

“Each operator has twin HRO wireless sets, one for the left ear and one for the right.” The Major went closer to the nearest operator and looked over his shoulder. He was intently scribbling in pencil on a pre-printed pad.

"MFDQY EOVEG PQEZB IUVCU ADWNY," read the Major to himself wondering what it could possibly mean. The boffins further up the line would have the job of cracking the code and making sense of it. This was the coal face, snatching the raw material from the enemy without them realising it. He hoped the hard work and dedication of the team of men in front of him would be duly acknowledged and rewarded when the time was right. The Major noticed a scoring on the pad by the letters RST.

"What's that?" said the Major pointing out what he was looking at to Mr Reardon.

"That's the RST Reporting System. The R is readability scoring from one unreadable to five perfectly readable. The S is Signal Strength ranging from one faint to nine very strong signals. The T is the tone of the signal from 1 a very rough hissing note to nine a pure DC note. Apparently the boffins want to know about the quality of the signals we are receiving."

One of the operators at the far end of the desk had removed his earphones and turned and asked Mr Reardon a question.

"On this Group Two sked," he said holding up a card he'd been given with the details of what he was expected to listen for, "Is that 1300 or 1500?" Mr Reardon looked at the handwriting and confirmed the time. The Major took the opportunity to jump in.

"Do you have a moment to talk?" he asked not wanting to interfere with the vital work that was being done.

"Yes sir, my next scheduled burst is not due for another fifteen minutes," he replied.

"How do you find your work?" asked the Major. The operator looked at Mr Reardon for confirmation he was free to answer this unknown soldier's questions. Mr Reardon nodded. "You may talk freely, Mr Rose," he said to the man dressed in civvies.

"It's a long time to concentrate but I enjoy radio work so it's not too bad," the operator said.

"What shifts do you do?" asked the Major.

"Usually we rotate over three eight hour shifts. I'm now on eight til four. The next shift do four until midnight and the night shift go from midnight until eight. Occasionally we might get a twelve hour shift. That's when the day seems long especially if the reception is not too good. Atmospherics, sir, can mess up the quality of the signal."

"Do you billet locally?" asked the Major.

"In the village, sir," he answered. "Very nice couple rent me a room."

"No problems there? Do they ask any awkward questions?"

"No problems sir. They don't ask. I did overhear them tell one relative that called their lodger was involved in hush hush work and they can't say anymore than that," replied Mr Rose.

"Very good," said the Major. "What do you do in your time off?" he asked wondering whether leisure time would be the area that would cause the greatest security threat. "What's the village pub like?"

"I wouldn't know, sir. I'm teetotal. Parents were strict Methodists. In my time off I sometimes walk down to the station to get a newspaper. Sometimes will cycle or catch the train into Penzance and have tea in Baileys or go to the Ritz Cinema. Or catch the train to St Ives for some fish and chips and a visit to the Royal Cinema." The answer left the Major wondering whether the security net on the operators' leisure time needed to be cast further afield than just the village. The Major had noticed a wooden rack containing a row of .303 rifles and a couple of American tommy guns. They were the focus of his next question.

"If the enemy came, which of the weapons would you go for to defend the wireless station?"

"Er, I'm, I'm not too sure sir," he replied hesitantly and on seeing the Major's quizzical expression added, "I've not had any weapons training, sir." The Major made a mental note as he thanked the operator and let him get back to his task, indicating to Mr Reardon it was time to move on. Outside with the view across part of St Ives Bay the Major asked how far they were from the coast and whether the station had any defence plans against raiders. He was told two miles and that the plans for invasion were to move as much equipment as they could before the enemy came and destroy anything they couldn't. Defence he was told was in the hands of the Home Guard locally and the forces in Hayle and along the coast. The Major wasn't reassured but it did spark a thought. If secret British installations on or close to the coast were not heavily defended, perhaps the German ones weren't either. He'd have to mention that idea to Churchill.

Chapter Fourteen

Mr Reardon suggested they next look at the two Direction Finding Stations. On learning that one was a mile or so up the lane, the Major offered to drive the chief interceptor in his car. Mr Reardon accepted gratefully. They turned left out of the field and went along Steppy Downs Road through the Home Guard roadblock on this side of the wireless station and followed it until it came out on the Hayle to Helston road. After going through St Erth Praze they again turned right along Conkers Road to Mably Farm. The Major was instructed to pull in by a gateway. The two men got out of the car and went through a small wooden pedestrian gate that had recently been inserted into the Cornish hedge with a concrete gate post.

Just inside the gate was a small concrete guard hut with a wooden earth closet behind it. About a quarter of the way into the field, there in the middle were two aerials attached to a beam which appeared to be on a central pivot.

"This is the Spaced Loop Station that we are trialling here at St Erth," said Mr Reardon as they walked across the grass towards the aerials. "The men have been struggling to get consistent results. The ability to rotate the aerials should help, as should having the receiver underground."

"Underground," repeated the Major wondering just what he was coming to look at.

"Yes, under the aerials is a large tank in which the operator sits. The aerials feed down through the central axle to the receiver," explained Mr Reardon. As they neared the site the

Major could make out a hatch in the ground. It consisted of a series of small Perspex glass windows. Mr Reardon reached down, tapped on the hatch and then slid the two halves to each side.

"James," he called down into the void. "I've brought a visitor to see you." He then preceded to climb down a ladder protruding out from the inside wall of the tank. The Major followed. Sat inside at a desk containing a wireless set, various other pieces of equipment and a telephone was the operator. James explained to the Major that he had one earphone attached to the landline. He was played a wireless signal down the line and with the other earphone connected to the radio set he had to match the two up. When they matched he would then get a direction bearing on the signal. He said that it was a bit slower than the Adcock system because they had to manually turn the beam with the aerials. The Major was still impressed.

Once back on the surface the Major asked Mr Reardon about security at the site.

"There's none," the Major said rather concerned. "It's a wireless station in a field with an unmanned sentry hut. Anyone could wander in here."

"It's hidden in plain sight," countered Mr Reardon. "The locals know they enter the field on pain of death, or at least a journey to the local police station. If someone got in the field, they most likely wouldn't know what they are looking at. The secret thing here is not the equipment, it's what we're doing with it."

“Which makes the security of your personnel all the more important,” argued the Major.

“The duty operator here has a direct phone line back to the site on St Erth Hill should any problems arise. The fact that he is rarely seen coming or going and is out of sight underground all the time in between, except when he needs to use the excuse me by the sentry hut, means that the odd farmworker or local travelling along the lane is not going to see too much to raise their curiosity.” The Major wasn’t convinced.

They drove back to St Erth Hill. En route a rattled Mr Reardon played his trump card.

“The only security scare we’ve had is when one of those boffins came down from London and stayed a while.”

“Oh yes?” said the Major curious as to what was coming.

“Man by the name of Lieutenant Trevor-Roper. He was visiting in the summer last year when he got taken ill. He spent some time in hospital here in Cornwall and then we arranged lodgings for him while he convalesced just down the lane with Mr and Mrs Taylor. Taylor’s a sergeant in the Home Guard and they’ve had several men from the wireless station lodge with them. Lieutenant Trevor-Roper suffers from erysipelas, his nose being particularly affected last year. Mrs Taylor helped nurse him.

“Anyway, when he was feeling a little better he decided to take himself off one day for an outing. It was the day Paris fell. Took the bus into Penzance and then decided to walk to Lamorna Cove. On his return, it seems he missed the bus from

Penzance and was walking back when someone became suspicious of him and alerted the Home Guard. They quickly improvised a roadblock ahead of him and stopped him armed with their double-barrelled shotgun. Suspicious of his spectacles and his accent they took him to the police where his papers were checked and he was released to continue his walk home. Fortunately for him the most suspicious thing he had in his possession was a copy of Divine Comedy by Dante."

"One can never be too careful," said the Major laughing. He had met the Oxford graduate, a native of Northumberland, a couple of times at various intelligence briefings and knew he could tease him with the story next time they bumped into each other. Mr Reardon was slightly irritated that the Major hadn't reacted to the story in the way he had hoped. The car pulled into the intercept station and the Major parked it outside the canteen hut.

"Our third site is across the lane," said Mr Reardon leading the way. On the left inside the gate was a concrete building. "That's the generator hut," said he continued. "It supplies us with electricity all hours of the day and night." They continued walking down the field to where a small hut and four aerials were situated inside a small round enclosure created by a wooden fence. They entered through a small gate in the fence. Cables ran from the hut to each of the aerials with a raised board to step on to avoid stepping on the cables. Once inside the hut they found another operator sitting at a wireless receiver. Mr Reardon made the introductions and then explained,

“This Direction Finding station uses the Adcock system. The four vertical aerials are fed into this instrument called a goniometer. It is an arrangement of two fixed coils, oriented at 90 degrees to each other, wound on an insulated form, with a smaller rotatable coil within that form. Each pair of diagonally opposite aerials are connected to one winding of the goniometer’s fixed coils. That has the effect of reproducing the electromagnetic field, sensed by the aerials, within the goniometer. So the movement is in the goniometer not with the aerials like the trial we are doing at the other site and so is much faster than manually moving the aerials. A signal from a German transmitter would be reproduced within the goniometer, and the rotor would sense a null signal in the direction of arrival, that is, pointing toward the transmitter. It is possible, if the signal is strong, to get a bearing within three to four seconds from first hearing the signal on the landline.” The Major listened intently. This was much more interesting than the science lessons he’d experienced at school over a decade ago.

“So we know just what the Germans are saying and where they are saying it,” he said.

“My last Group 2 hit came from the suburbs of Berlin,” said Cornish, the operator. If he was hoping for some enlightenment as to what this was from the Major he was disappointed as the Major was not going to reveal he had pinpointed the wireless transmitter for many of the Abwehr’s services. Thus if an enemy raid did capture any of the personnel they would have no idea what it was they were listening to and so couldn’t reveal that easily to the interrogator. There was also less chance of a security breach within this country increasing the risk of word getting back to Germany. The Daily Mirror had been very heavily sat on by Admiral George Thompson, the Chief Press Censor, after its first editions on the morning of Friday 14th February had run a story exposing the fact that Voluntary Interceptors were tapping Nazi Morse Code.

"Keep up the good work," said the Major as he patted the operator on the shoulder and turned to leave the hut. Mr Reardon had just stepped outside when two rifle shots rang out. As he followed Mr Reardon out the Major's hand instinctively moved towards his holster. The sound seemed to have come from over the hedge to the north and the two men scanned their horizon for sight of any explanation. Just then a Home Guard soldier appeared at the gate at the top of the field and came running down towards them. He was breathless when he arrived.

"Intruder," he said between gasps. "Wearing a light brown coat.... Young man..... Ran off into the next field... when we challenged him.... Both shot at him.... Don't think we hit him....Hart has followed him down next field.... Was climbing hedge so I came in here.... Matthews has gone on the bike to call out the platoon."

The Major said to Mr Reardon, "Sound the alert for your men. Any spare, get them armed and patrol your field perimeter. Go!" Mr Reardon disappeared back into the nearby hut and having explained to Ben Cornish headed back up the slope towards the lane. The Major pointed towards a gate a little further down the field and said to the Home Guard,

"Let's go through there and see if we can see him." They set off at a run but the Home Guard was soon lagging behind the young and athletic Major. The Major arrived in the gateway first and scanned the field but could see nothing other than a gorse covered mound of old mine waste in the middle of the field. When the Home Guard arrived he shouted,

"There he is!" The Major looked and emerging into view was the fugitive heading for the gate in the far corner of the field. "He's heading out towards Porthcollum Lane," said the Home Guard but the Major was already several paces away giving chase. The Major moved down into the field so the mound wouldn't again block his view and was running as fast as the freshly ploughed soil would allow him. As the intruder fled through the gateway the Major saw there was only a small neck of land before the next gateway. He saw the fugitive hesitate and then turn right and disappear out of sight.

Chapter Fifteen

The Major glanced back and his Home Guard companion was already some sixty yards behind. He knew it would be no good to wait so he kept running. When he got out to the lane he turned right and found the lane turned a sharp left almost immediately. He was now running downhill for which he was grateful but knew it would also give a boost to the man they were chasing. The lane soon came to a junction. Off to the right the lane went uphill and the Major guessed it must go back towards the lane the wireless intercept station was on. He knew if he were the fugitive he would not head that way as that was the lane where the Home Guard had their roadblock. So he took the bridleway off to the left. It continued to go downhill but it was not made up. After a couple of sharp bends and a few more twists and turns the Major came to a straighter section and in the distance he could see his quarry. The Major was pleased he had gained slightly on his man and it spurred him on. His lungs were now bursting and he was hoping to get his second wind.

The fugitive soon stopped and glanced left and right. He'd obviously come to a junction and was deciding which way to go. He disappeared off to the right. It was several moments before the Major reached the same spot. He saw that the lane bent sharply to the left and looked as it headed down towards a farm. An even rougher track continued on in front of him. To the right there was a stone style in the hedge and that's where he turned. The path ran alongside the hedge at the bottom of the field. The Major scanned the field to make sure his man had not veered off the path. There was no sign of him so he kept going. Through the next gap in the Cornish hedgerow he caught a brief glimpse of the man running about a field and a half ahead of him. He seemed to have taken his coat off as he was now carrying it over his arm. The Major sensed this was no accidental intruder who had caused the Home Guard to open fire. While he knew there had been a few incidents around the country where they had been trigger happy, no casual walker would sustain a flight of this length. His quarry must be young and fit.

In the next field the path veered diagonally across the field and the Major soon found himself out on another tarmacadamed lane. There were now on the floor of the valley and the Major guessed the stream would now form a barrier to his fugitive so he headed up the lane which he felt must take him towards the village. He was right and was soon passing the parish church. He then caught a glimpse through the trees of his quarry running up the road on the other side of the river. At least the Major knew now which way to turn at the crossroads.

He passed the School Rooms and turned left over the bridge. A mother with a young child was crossing the bridge and both looked at the Major somewhat concerned and wondering what was going on given the young man they had passed running up the hill just a few moments ago. The Major's pace slowed as the gradient steepened. He had deduced by now the fugitive must be heading for either the railway station or the A30. He had enough of a view up Tredrea Lane to be confident his quarry had turned right towards Treloweth. He kept going wondering where the Home Guard were, especially the lad who had cycled to the village to raise the alarm. The Major wondered if he might have been wiser going for his car instead of pursuing the fugitive but concluded the Home Guard soldier he'd left behind would have lost his man in the first couple of fields. Now there was nothing for it but to keep going especially as he heard in the distance the sound of a train approaching from the west..

The Major ran through the dip and headed up towards the railway bridge. There was no sign of his quarry but he sensed he would be seeking to make his getaway by train. Instead of heading under the railway bridge the Major decided to take a short cut to the station. He went to the right hand parapet, pulled himself up onto the wall and then clambered up the steep slope of bricks to the metal girder bridge, swung his leg over the rail and in no time was walking along the down platform. The train he had heard approaching was now pulling away, so he sprinted over the footbridge onto the platform the train had just left and grabbed a startled porter.

“Young man, blonde hair, carrying a coat,” puffed the Major. “Did he get on that train?”

“I saw two elderly ladies, a sailor and a dairy worker get on. No blonde young man,” replied the bemused porter. The Major then heard a guard's whistle and realised the St Ives train was about to leave. He turned, ran down the couple of steps onto the lower platform and as the guard was about to wave his green flag to signal for the driver he rushed for the open guard's door and jumped on. Before the guard could protest the Major had disappeared through the door from his compartment and into the corridor of the train. The Major sighed.

"At least it was a bit easier to catch than trains at Padstow," he thought to himself remembering his flying leap last summer. He looked up the corridor. 'A bit easier than clambering over trucks!' Usually the St Ives local trains consisted of two coaches without corridors but after the bombing of the train in Falmouth there was a shortage of rolling stock and so the summer coaches were brought out and pressed into service. Thus this train had two composite corridor coaches as well as the composite brake coach pulled by Prairie engine 4549. So if the Major was going to catch his man, assuming he was on the train, he would have to check every compartment within the four mile journey.

The first two compartments after the guard's berth were first class but that didn't stop the Major opening the door to check on the passengers and the luggage rack. The passengers said nothing noticing the uniform. In the second a lady in a large hat was in the midst of asking,

"What is that building, my dear Terrence?" Before Terrence had a chance to answer the Major spoke.

"That's the dairy where they make Ennis Vale butter, ma'am. All well here?" The startled couple just nodded, speechless at the unusual intrusion as the Major continued on his way. The next four compartments revealed an assortment of travellers and one empty compartment but no fugitive. Next was the toilet. The Major tried the handle. It was locked. He knocked.

"Just a moment," came the cry from within. The Major waited glancing out the window as the train had passed under the A30 and over the St Ives road and was now alongside the River

Hayle. Fortunately the tide was in and so the vast expanse of mud was covered. The train had almost reached Lelant station by the time the elderly gentleman appeared. He looked confused as the waiting Major headed off into the next coach rather than using the facility.

In the next coach the first lavatory was empty as was the first compartment. As he got to the next compartment the blinds had been pulled down so it was not possible to see into the compartment. Undeterred the Major opened the door and stepped in to find a couple of Royal Engineers engaged in amorous activities with a couple of Land Army girls. One of the girls screamed at the intrusion and her soldier coughed and spluttered at the sight of such a senior officer, but by the time the other two had pulled themselves apart the Major was long gone.

The train passed the golden sands of Porth Kidney with its terrific views across the bay to Godrevy with its lighthouse. On the rocks at Gwithian overlooking the lighthouse the St Ives lifeboat had washed up back in January 1939 when in a ferocious storm it had capsized several times and seven of the crew perished. Only William Freeman survived – the only man not ready to meet his Maker that night. It had been his first outing in the boat and he volunteered at the last moment when the crew were one short as they launched at three o'clock in the morning. Thirteen children had been left without a father. It was the second lifeboat St Ives had lost within twelve months. The faith, bravery and sacrifice of those who died made a significant impact in the small fishing community.

The Major spotted a couple of the pillboxes on the dunes and knew any attempt by his fugitive to jump off at this point would be foolhardy. As the train slowed to stop at Carbis Bay the Major had just one coach left to check. He paused his searching to put his head out of a window on the side without a platform just to make sure no one jumped off onto the grass bank. As the guard's whistle blew he rushed to the other side to check on the passengers making their way up the steep footpath to the station exit. There were only two and his quarry was not one of them.

He continued his search into the final carriage. He had another delay as he waited to check the toilet. He was halfway along when the train came to a stand at the home signal before the final descent into St Ives station. Again the Major paused to make sure no one escaped from the train during its momentary halt. He managed one more compartment before the train pulled into the long platform. Before the train had come to a stop the front door of the carriage was thrown open and a young man with blonde hair stepped off and began to run towards the town.

The Major had alighted at the door half way along the coach and by the time he had spotted the fugitive several people had got out onto the platform. The Major started to run dodging round one couple and then a child and that's when a zealous porter with a trolley coming to help with the passenger's luggage caught him. The lip of the trolley clipped the Major's ankle and he fell. He was winded but not seriously hurt. Several people rushed to his aid and helped him up. The porter was extremely apologetic. The Major assured him no harm was done and turned to run. The Major could see his quarry in the distance. His ankle throbbed as he ran. He saw the fugitive disappear down the steps towards Pedn Olva. By the time he got to the top of the steps the Major glanced over the wall and he saw his fugitive's face for the first time. It was a face etched into his memory after the last time the two of them had met at close quarters. The recognition was mutual in that split second. Incensed that Johann had the audacity to return to Cornwall the Major tore down the steps as fast as he could. He turned to head along the Warren but here there were a larger number of people which made his progress slow. By the time he had reached the Cuddy he had lost his man completely. He went up to the corner by the old fire station but there was no sight of the young blonde haired man in any direction.

For a further half an hour the Major wandered the narrow streets of St Ives in the hope of spotting him again. Despondent he gave up and headed for the police station in Will's Lane. John, the police sergeant, noted down the description of the wanted man but told the Major he did not think they would be able to do a lot as there was now only himself, a constable and the war reserves making up the police force of St Ives. He bemoaned the number of people who used the beaches dressed suitably for the sunny weather but not an identity card in sight and not the resources to enforce even that basic security measure.

The Major asked if there were any Fifth Columnists in the town. The sergeant didn't know of any despite various rumours. The Major wondered whether his collision with the porter was an accident or if there was anything more sinister to it. After all, before the war, von Ribbentrop, when he was the German ambassador in London, had spent several holidays in Cornwall and had even stayed at the Tregenna Castle Hotel in St Ives. Had he made connections on his visits? Were there those who were either sympathetic to the Nazi cause or were in the pay of the enemy? The Major sensed Johann had to be having help within the county but alerting the local police was all he could do for now.

It was an exhausted Major who trudged up the hill to the station, bought a ticket for the journey back to St Erth and waited for the next train. Gazing out at the deep blue sea, a clear sky and the panoramic view of the bay it was hard to believe there was a war on. But at war they clearly were as his chase with Johann, the supposed Dutchman, showed. The Major churned everything over in his mind. 'What had brought Johann back? What was he doing at St Erth? Were the Germans aware of what was going on there or was he just sniffing around? Where was he based? Who was helping him? How had they not picked up the Abwehr wireless traffic to alert them to his arrival? How did he get here? How long has he been here? With whom is he communicating?'

"To ask the hard questions is simple," wrote Auden. The train arrived and the Major boarded and chose a seaward seat. If he had no answers for now, at least he'd enjoy the view. The Major knew his visit to Cornwall had just taken on a new dynamic and he would have to report in to London. He sunk into the dusty seat in the train and headed back to the wireless intercept station.

Chapter Sixteen

It was a concerned Johann that arrived back in Bar Road that evening. He had walked in a circuitous route from the station just to make sure he was not being followed. Now he walked the length of the road and back again before venturing up the path into his lodgings to be certain he was not being watched. He was exhausted from his exertions and would be glad of his bed assuming his troubled mind would let him sleep.

He had concluded that the wireless station was nothing significant as it was only being protected by the Home Guard and not regular troops. But what was that English Major doing there? Was it just coincidence? Or was there something he had missed? Were they on to him once more? The Major had come close to ruining his last mission and he did not want him interfering again. How did the Major know he was here? How did that infernal Englishman know Johann was visiting St Erth on a day when he should have been working in the dockyard? Had his cover been blown? Were they tracking him to see where he would go and who his contacts were? He would need to lay low for a couple of days and see if anything developed. It was back to work tomorrow after his 'day of bed rest ordered by the doctor'.

Johann learned from Mrs Browning that there were no messages or callers for him in his absence. She merely assumed he had been at work and he did not enlighten her otherwise. Jones was nowhere to be seen. Johann took the opportunity of an early night. After tossing and turning for a while he had finally dropped off through sheer exhaustion only to be awoken at five to eleven by the air raid siren. He groaned and decided if he were to die from a German bomb then it would at least be in the warmth and comfort of his bed. Avoiding the shelter proved to be a sound choice as the alert went on for four hours and not a single bomb was dropped. The Luftwaffe were flying north; Cornwall was not the target for tonight.

The Major's phone call to London was not one he enjoyed. He was told that his trip to Cornwall would be extended so he could coordinate the round up of the enemy agent working with the security service, the local police and any military resources deemed necessary to do the job. Until they had some firm leads to go on he was ordered to continue with his review of the security arrangements of as many Cornish military installations as he could manage. The security service would do a sweep of all its known persons of interest and sites of concern to see if the agent would break cover. The police would circulate details of the wanted man to all their police stations. Details were to be kept quiet from the public at this stage so as not to cause alarm.

Wednesday morning had been a morning of phone calls and so the Major was pleased to get out in his car that afternoon. He was headed to Perranporth and a small top secret installation nestled on the cliff at Droskyn point. He had taken the St Agnes road so he could approach Perranporth from the west and get a glimpse of the new airfield that had just become operational last month. From the road he got sight of the new hard runway that had been built. At the Cligga end of the site there was a marquee tent and an old mine building that was being used as the watch tower. The Major spotted a couple of Spitfires at this end of the runway. They were Mark IIA's and had been fitted with long range fuel tanks for operations defending the Western Approaches. On one he saw the LZ squadron code which identified that 66 Squadron were in residence.

As he approached St George's Farm he could see a half constructed pillbox. Apart from the sentry box the other side of the farm and the brand new perimeter fence, that was all the defences of the new airfield he could make out. However, he also knew that the two hundred foot cliffs on the seaward side would act as a deterrent to any attacker. He drove down St George's Hill and turned left onto Beach Road. As he approached the beach he could see the Promenade was covered in barbed wire. The ramp down to the beach was blocked by an anti-tank wall. On the beach itself a barricade of scaffolding ran from the Promenade Hotel steps across the beach to the flat rocks at Cotty's Point where there was a Type 24 pillbox by the Wheal Mary adit. As he climbed the hill he could see there were two more pillboxes, one at beach level and one atop the small cliff in front of Ponsmere House.

The Major drove past the Droskyn Castle Hotel where two RAF officers were emerging from the front door, having been billeted in the building designed by Silvanus Trevail. The Major then turned right along the narrow lane that ran out towards the point. Partway along he ran into a gate with a sentry posted. Having checked the Major's papers, the sailor opened the gate and let the Major drive in for he had arrived at AES Perranporth. The Admiralty Experimental Station was an outpost of the

Admiralty Research Laboratory. It was the main site in the UK for underwater acoustic experiments such as underwater acoustic propagation and transducer investigations.

After the introductions the Major was shown some of the work they were currently doing on ASDIC – anti-submarine detection. He was taken down a path on the cliff slope to a small hut from which cables were fed down the cliff and into the sea. It was explained that these were connected to hydrophones some distance out from the shore and were being used to detect both submarine and surface vessel approaches. The research was designed to improve the detection of enemy craft and help with noise reduction on British craft. The Major was impressed by the clear and succinct way one of the civilians on the team, a Mr Francis Crick, was able to explain the detail on hydrophonics.

The Major discussed their defence strategies which in the main consisted of destroying equipment and records in the event of a raid or invasion, standard naval procedures for any vessel that was in danger of being captured or sunk. The cliffs and the defences of Perranporth itself were the main deterrent to the enemy and given that during an alert the hydrophones would be on, the Station would have some warning of a seaborne arrival. The Station was controlled by D Group, the ARL's Acoustic Group.

Feeling satisfied with his visit the Major decided he would treat himself to a cup of tea in Perranporth before the return journey. He drove down the hill and pulled up outside the Men's Institute in Beach Road. Next to the Institute was an ice cream shop and dairy that also had a café. Served by the proprietor

Samuel Keast, the Major indulged in a custard tart to go with his cup of Lyons tea.

Elizabeth knew she would be glad to get back to the barracks in Bodmin. Firstly she was happier driving cars than being the passenger in one, especially as this was Mr Thomas' hearse. It was a sad duty she had been called on to perform. A soldier from a regiment based in Newquay had died in the Emergency Hospital in Bodmin and someone from the army was requested to accompany the body as it was taken back to his regiment for burial. Elizabeth didn't know quite how she had landed up with the duty but the Depot seemed to be tied up with some exercise and so the ATS were drafted in.

On the outward journey Mr Thomas had been rather quiet and sombre, performing his duties with the decorum and dignity that his profession required. The soldier had been guarding an anti-aircraft post at Hemmick Beach on the south coast at the weekend when it was bombed by a German aircraft. One soldier had been killed outright and Private Wilson and an auxiliary coastguard from Gorran Haven had been seriously injured. They had been brought to the hospital in Bodmin which occupied the Kendall Building in the St Lawrence's Hospital complex but both had died from their wounds within twenty four hours. The soldiers had served with the Duke of Wellington's Regiment and Elizabeth felt for the families back in Yorkshire.

On the return journey Mr Thomas had been rather more talkative. Elizabeth learned that his company had the funeral directors contract with the DCLI Depot and Mr Thomas had a soft spot for the soldier who had had too much too drink and had on several occasions put them in his hearse and driven them back into barracks as the car was known on the gate and no questions were asked when it passed through with the curtains in the rear drawn shut. That way a number of soldiers had escaped the punishment for returning to barracks the worse the wear for drink. Elizabeth didn't know whether to smile or to report Mr Thomas to her commanding officer. She decided in the words of Falstaff 'Discretion was the better part of valour.'

The rest of the Major's week was filled with visits to small secret installations in seemingly out of the way places. He had visited a couple of War Office Direction Finding posts at Chacewater, one High Frequency, the other Medium Frequency, used by the army to triangulate enemy stations. He'd been down to Coverack to visit the Royal Navy's Home Defence Unit and their Direction Finding station at St Just in Penwith. For the RAF he had visited their Direction Finding stations at Land's End and above Pendeen on Woon Gumpus Common. He had paid visits to the new Chain Home Low radar stations at Hor's Point near Hellesveor above St Ives and Mark's Castle at Land's End where to his surprise he found the Land's End Hotel still open and was able to enjoy a good meal before continuing his journey.

It was during his visit to the Naval Wireless Station at Land's End that the Major learned some alarming news. Bismarck, the new German battleship, had sailed from Norway and was heading for the Atlantic. The Navy was using a vast number of resources to try to locate her and prevent her getting anywhere near the North Atlantic convoy routes. The small station was a hive of activity as the search for the needle in the haystack continued and messages were relayed back and forth. The Major kept his visit brief so as not to be too much of a distraction.

On the Saturday the Major drove up to Bodmin for a meeting with the Chief Constable of the Cornwall Constabulary. Major Edgar Hare was a Duke of Cornwall's Light Infantry veteran from the Great War and ran his police force with a military precision that saw him respected by both officer and civilians alike. He was a tall, slim man with a firm fixed face but a warm handshake as he welcomed the Major into his office. The Major briefed him on the situation with the enemy agent known as Johann and thought to be posing as a Dutchman. The Chief Constable remembered reading the reports on the events of last summer and was surprised the same character had returned. He outlined to the Major what the police had done since Superintendent Rowland of the Camborne Division had reported to headquarters following the Major's original notification at St Ives. The two men discussed what else could be done and came up with a couple of suggestions that the security service could follow up, but the best chance of success would be brought about by vigilance for when the agent broke cover again.

As the congenial meeting drew to its conclusion the Chief Constable revealed that the next issue he had to deal with was reports of lights being shone on the hills above the aerodrome at St Eval during the spate of recent Luftwaffe bombing raids.

"We've had three reports from two different people claiming to have seen lights up on Trelow Downs during the recent air raids. The concern is that a Fifth Columnist is signalling to the enemy planes," explained the Chief Constable. The Major laughed and the policeman was taken aback at the reaction. "What's so funny?" he asked somewhat annoyed.

"If you had an aerodrome that was regularly being attacked how could you protect your airfield?" asked the Major.

"I'd have lots of anti-aircraft guns and barrage balloons," said the policeman.

"Both of which are vital but only reveal the location to the enemy," said the Major.

"But how can you hide an airfield?" asked Major Hare.

"How well do you know your Henry V?" asked the Major. He then began to quote Act III of Shakespeare's play.

"*In peace, there's nothing so becomes a man,*
As modest stillness and humility;
But when the blast…."

The Major tailed off as the Chief Constable took up the quote.

"*…The blast of war blows in our ears,*
Then imitate the action of a tiger."

It took a moment for the penny to drop. "You mean, they are imitating an airfield up there on the Downs?"

"The enemy bomber works by dropping his bombs where he sees the first ones hit, so if we light some fires and show a few lights that look like an airfield under attack we can draw their bombs away from the real aerodrome to the imitation one," explained the Major.

"Ingenious," said the policeman absolutely amazed. "So the reports are genuine. There are lights on the Downs during a raid but they are to fool the enemy and not to help him. But what poor devil is there operating those lights trying to make the Germans drop bombs on his head?"

"That's Corporal in Charge Jim Cant and his airmen. When he gets a call from ops, they dash along a flarepath of about twenty Gooseneck flares with a box of matches and light them. The enemy then thinks it's the flarepath at St Eval and so targets the decoy site. The airmen then scurry back to their control bunker before the bombs start dropping."

"I'm going to have to tell my men in the local area," said Major Hare.

"Not a problem as long as they realise it's all hush-hush," replied the Major. "They've now built a second one up on Tregonetha Downs. That's got electric lights so the men can sit in their bunker and just throw a switch."

"Amazing!" The police chief was truly gobsmacked. "Who thought of this?"

"That's Colonel Turner's Department," replied the Major. "They are based at Shepperton Studios and employ a number of experts from the film industry. They have built dummy airfields, factories and even towns at various places around the country."

"I take my hat off to them, and especially the men who operate the sites," said Major Hare genuinely impressed. "I am so glad you've told me this. It has saved a lot of police time investigating these reports of lights and chasing the non-existent shadows of a Fifth Columnist on the Downs above St Eval."

"Happy to be of service. All the more effort to be put into catching the agent who is on the loose," said the Major.

"I assure you we will do all that we can," said the Chief Constable standing up. The Major shook his outstretched hand and promised to keep in touch.

Two hours later the Major was tucking into a plate of Mrs Rickard's stew. It was a quiet evening at home with his parents during which the Major's thoughts strayed to Elizabeth and the lovely evening they had enjoyed this time last week. He wondered what she was doing now. He had been tempted to barge into the barracks again but knew he could only push his luck with Sergeant Buscombe so far. He had heard nothing from Elizabeth so reluctantly had driven straight back from Bodmin.

After a game of cards with his father, Mr Trevennel had risen and switched on the wireless for the BBC's Home Service special Empire Day programme 'Brothers In Arms' that recalled the story of the war through the summer of 1940 and ended with the sentiment "The sea made us and the sea will keep us."

The Major listened in silence thinking it was a story only half told.

Next came the Nine O'clock News after the chimes of Big Ben. The opening headlines shocked the Trevennel family.

"HMS Hood is sunk." The announcer's words were like a sledgehammer. "The ship was sunk by a lucky strike on her magazine which exploded." The pride of the British Navy and its gallant crew were lost. Although none of them knew any of the crew it was almost as if the loss of this ship was personal. The mood was sombre as they stayed and listened to the Empire Day concert. The stirring notes of Purcell's 'Trumpet Voluntary' seemed to spell out a determination that the ship would be avenged, that there would be a day of reckoning for the Bismarck. The 'Fantasia of British Sea Songs' played by the BBC Orchestra conducted by Henry J. Wood was a fitting tribute to those young lives lost in the waters of the Denmark Strait.

As he went to bed the Major wondered just what this portended for Britain as she faced invasion, a serious setback in the Battle of the Atlantic, a raging battle in Crete as the Mediterranean War hung in the balance. Even the bombing of the House of Commons earlier in the month seemed to symbolise that democracy was fighting for its life. Britain was alone. Would she survive?

Chapter Seventeen

Elizabeth collapsed back onto her bed in the barrack room. It was the last bit of news she wanted to hear. It had been a lousy Monday. The weather had changed and had been bad all day. She had got all greasy sorting out the engine on one of the staff cars. A couple of the ATS girls had fallen out and she had had to read them both the riot act in order to nip the impact it could have on the whole unit in the bud. Now she had this scribbled note from the Major which had been handed in at the gate. She looked at the piece of paper again as the tears welled up in her eyes.

"Dear Elizabeth," it read. "I hope you are well. Duty has called me back to London for a meeting. Not sure when I will be back but I am hoping it will be sooner rather than later. Just wanted to let you know so I didn't disappear without trace. Yours as always, Zac."

'At least he has had the courtesy to let me know which in his job is difficult,' she reasoned with herself. 'But there's no knowing when he will be back and there's so much I want to tell him. But was this his way of saying "Goodbye"? There was no declaration of his feelings,' she despaired. "But he did say "Yours as always" and he's hoping to be back soon,' she countered. 'Oh I don't know,' she thought and threw the letter on the chair beside her bed. 'Why did the path of true love never run smooth?'

She had a restless night. Sleep was hard to come by and when it did it was full of dreams of Zac in the arms of another woman. She tried telling herself she was being stupid but that made no difference and she was almost grateful when the distant sounds of the bugler sounding reveille meant she could head into the showers.

Not even the news on the mess wireless that the Bismarck had been sunk could lift her out her despondency. The avenging of the Hood was the talk of the mess and several asked for her opinion on it and all she could say was she was sorry for the families of all the young men who have died in the icy waters of the Atlantic in the past week. No one in the ATS knew she had lost a fiancé on the Royal Oak in Scapa Flow in 1939, but it all added to the black clouds that seemed to engulf her. The only distraction was her work and she threw herself into her duties with a resolution that in the words of Jack Hylton's song, "Blue skies were around the corner."

It was a difficult day for Johann. Only at the weekend he had felt triumphant as he listened with Mr and Mrs Browning to the BBC reporting the loss of the Hood. Now just three days later there was a wave of euphoria that swept through the workforce in the dockyard as the news broke of the chase and final destruction of the Bismarck. He had to hide his true feelings as he spent the afternoon working in the Plater's Shop. He was glad when the shift was over and he could leave.

Back at the lodging Mrs Browning was full of the news. Johann avoided making comment and said he was heading out for the evening. He had decided he would take a walk around Falmouth and try and locate all the sites of the balloon barrage. He had already established that 959 Squadron RAF were in charge of the sites and with the inclement weather the balloons were more likely to be on their beds and so much easier to identify the site.

Three hours later having walked a good number of miles but without raising too much suspicion Johann had a list of fourteen noted down. There were a couple more on the Trefusis or St Mawes side of the water but they would have to wait for another occasion. He was amazed at the choice of sites the RAF had made. One was in the Grammar School field, another in a sports club field, a third just below the golf course. By following a couple of RAF chaps at a distance he discovered they were based at the Gwendra Hotel, a fine 45 bedroom hotel on Cliff Road. He felt it had been a worthwhile evening and served to lift his spirits. He had only been asked for his papers once when he'd bumped into some Home Guard at the crossroads near Marlborough House and they were quickly satisfied that all was in order. He was satisfied that no one was tailing him and his concerns about the Major from their chase at St Erth and St Ives had largely abated.

He had just returned to the house in Bar Road shortly after ten o'clock and made himself a drink when the air raid siren went. He took his cup with him into the shelter. He was grateful because it was gone midnight before the all clear sounded. He fell off to sleep thinking of and planning for future opportunities for mischief at the dockyard.

It was against her better judgement or so she felt that Elizabeth agreed to go with a couple of the ATS girls to the dance that was being held in the Centenary Rooms next to the

Methodist Church in Bodmin. She wasn't in the mood for dancing and spent the first half of the evening chatting to a diminutive lass called Monica in Civil Defence uniform who was celebrating having just passed the course for becoming a local ARP instructor. When a corporal in the Royal Engineers asked her for her dance and insisted he wouldn't take a refusal, Elizabeth got to her feet and joined the dance floor. The first dance was a foxtrot and apart from the poor fellow having two left feet Elizabeth coped with the experience. Over the next couple of dances as the corporal began to leer more and more and become freer with his hands, Elizabeth decided it was time for an early night. She made her excuses and headed out into the night.

She hadn't gone far down the road from the Assembly Rooms when footsteps came scurrying up behind her.

"If you're running out on me, then at least let me walk you home," said the lanky corporal.

"I am perfectly capable of walking myself home, thank you very much," replied Elizabeth tersely.

"Don't be like that. I am only trying to be friendly," he said feigning hurt.

"Too friendly from what you were trying in there," said an indignant Elizabeth.

"Can't a soldier have a friendly squeeze while he's having a dance?" asked the soldier.

“Not with my rear,” said Elizabeth disliking the man more and more as the conversation continued.

“No harm intended,” said the man lamely as if that were some kind of defence. “Well, we’re headed in the same direction so we may as well walk together.” The corporal was certainly persistent.

“If you must,” said Elizabeth begrudgingly. “But know that I’m stepping out with an officer and a gentleman, so I have no desire for your attentions.” The mention of the fact made her mind wander to the Major and she was grateful that he was a far finer character than this smarmy soldier. By the time they had reached the Town Arms Hotel Elizabeth had come up with a dozen reasons why she preferred the Major to this obnoxious corporal although she didn’t share her insights. He was havering on about something but Elizabeth wasn’t listening. Her mind was on greater things. She was grateful when he suddenly said his goodbyes and crossed the road and went into the shoe shop that had a shell hanging up outside it. The shop had been commandeered by the Royal Engineers Bomb Disposal Squad. Elizabeth was so relieved at his early departure that she decided to stop in the YMCA under the Public Rooms and have a cocoa. It was one of the treats that the YMCA run by Len White of Castle Street provided for the troops.

With her spirits fortified she continued the journey back to the Depot up the long haul of St Nicholas Street, but she didn’t notice the hill or the distance as her mind wandered to memories of the happy times she had spent with the Major. The evening had made her miss him even more and she decided she would write him a quick letter before going to bed.

"Troubles may come but troubles will go," she hummed to herself as she passed the railway station. "Blue skies are round the corner, everything's going to be right."

Chapter Eighteen

It was Saturday 28th June before the Major finally returned to Cornwall. The intervening weeks had seemed like an eternity to Elizabeth but the exchange of letters between them had been positive and encouraging and cleared the air of the doubts the two of them seemed to have following the weekend at the Trevennel's home at Bosvarren. They were not going to let faith, family or the fortunes of war stand between them and while there were still questions to be resolved it was with a renewed determination to work them through that the two were looking forward to some time together over the weekend. The Major had written to say he had booked two rooms at the Pentargon Hotel on the sea front at Falmouth for Saturday and Sunday night and although Elizabeth would have to travel back by train early on Monday morning, the Major would pick her up on the Saturday on his way down from London. He had also assured Elizabeth that although the hotel had been taken over by the army there were also Wrens accommodated there so she would not be the only female.

Elizabeth had been able to secure a forty eight hour pass to enable her to be away for the weekend. Some negotiation with Sergeant Buscombe had allowed the timings of that to be adjusted so she could travel back on the Monday morning. She was sure her commanding officer would call in the favours she'd stacked up one day, or perhaps her Sergeant thought it might be worth having the Major as her ally sometime. Elizabeth had spent the afternoon getting herself ready. Her uniform was ironed, her hair brushed endlessly and her overnight bag packed three times.

It was just after four o'clock when Bunny stuck her head round the door and smiled.

"He's here. Have a spiffing time. Don't do anything I wouldn't, mind," she said with a grin.

"That leaves me a lot of scope," retorted Elizabeth grabbing her bag and coat and following Bunny down the stairs. Outside, stood by his car, was the Major looking as handsome as Elizabeth had ever seen him. He'd had a haircut since they were last together and the tidy look suited him. He took her bag and coat and put them in the back. Elizabeth slid into the passenger seat. The Major got behind the wheel, started the car and drove towards the gate onto Lostwithiel Road. The sentry saluted as they passed wondering how this Major had managed to steal the best looking woman on the base.

"You look adorable," said the Major as they pulled across the road and headed over the railway bridge.

"Thank you," replied Elizabeth smiling with her blue eyes gazing at the Major. "You're looking pretty dapper yourself."

"One has to make an effort for the most beautiful woman in Cornwall," he grinned as he changed gear for the car to pull up the hill over the Beacon. They were soon on the A30 and heading for Redruth where they would turn off onto the Falmouth road, not that they noticed the miles as the conversation flowed as they shared all that had been happening over the last month. The topics ranged from the German attack against Russia (the reason the Major had been recalled to London for intelligence briefings prior to the German onslaught) to the death of Kaiser Wilhelm II in Holland, the introduction of clothes rationing at the beginning of the month to the plane to the Isles of Scilly disappearing without trace. They had talked of barrack room hilarity to the state of London after the May blitz, of news of Elizabeth's family on the farm just outside Padstow and the visit by an official from the War Agricultural Committee who had somehow managed to trip over in the pig sty and get himself covered from head to toe to the Major's parents and of the announcement by the Air Chief Marshal of the role radio location had played in winning the Battle of Britain last year.

The last few miles down into Falmouth were slow as they fell in behind a convoy of trucks bringing supplies to Falmouth. It was just before six when the Major pulled into the drive at the back of the hotel and brought the car to a stop in front of the door. Mr Price, the proprietor came out to greet them, and showed them inside. After completing the formalities at the desk, they were then shown to their rooms which were on the top floor either side of the central staircase.

Elizabeth, after hanging up her coat, decided that unpacking could wait until later and strolled across the landing and knocked on the Major's door.

"Come in," he said in an officious tone, as if he were expecting Mr Price to return. His face broke into a broad smile when he realised that it was Elizabeth that was entering. He strode across the room and wrapped his arms round her and swept her off her feet in an enormous hug.

"I've missed you," he said tenderly and as Elizabeth's feet finally touched the ground again he leant forward and kissed her. She responded in kind and their lips entwined in a passionate embrace that neither wanted to end.

"Dinner is at seven," said the Major when the moment concluded. Elizabeth strode to the window and looked out at the view of the bay.

"Just making sure your room hasn't got a better view than mine," she said turning back with a smile. "That's the one thing I miss in Bodmin," she said looking back out the window.

"Me?" said the Major knowing he wouldn't be the answer.

"That too," said Elizabeth grinning. "No, the sea. I miss the sea. From the farm we could see the tide come in and out every day. There's something humbling about watching the sea, don't you think?" she asked.

"I guess when you see it's mighty power then, yes, it's humbling. But it's like a mill pond out there today," said the Major.

At seven the Major and Elizabeth were seated in the dining room. There were separate tables for all the guests allowing a greater degree of privacy, even if the clientele were mostly a mix of army officers and Wrens. No doubt several were wondering who the dashing couple were at the table in the corner. Miss Margaret Jerome was the resident hostess for the dinner and the entertainment that followed in the comfortable lounge. The well known BBC artiste Pauline Crothers entertained the residents and guests of the hotel with her violin solos assisted at the piano by her husband Mr Paine. The items were interspersed with community singing of a range of wartime and old time favourites and everyone had an enjoyable hour.

A nightcap was served and when Elizabeth expected the Major to suggest they retire he instead proposed they go for a walk along the sea front. It wasn't a cold night and as the last vestiges of light faded in the west the two of them walked along Cliff Road to Gyllyngvase Beach. They passed several service personnel coming and going from their duties but none bothered the happy couple as they sauntered along hand in hand.

"Come on, let's go for a paddle," said the Major with a mischievous grin.

"You serious?" said Elizabeth looking at the scaffolding and barbed wire that stretched across the beach.

"Yes, we can climb through that. It's not mined, so it's perfectly safe," said the Major. So Elizabeth duly ducked and weaved as the Major held apart the barbed wire that was twisted round the steel scaffolding poles and the two of them made their way to the water's edge where they took off their socks and shoes, rolled their trousers up to the knee and stepped into the cold water.

The Major bent down to splash Elizabeth but she saw what he was up to.

"Don't you even think about it. You don't know how long I spent on my hair today and getting it sticky and matted with salt water will not please me one bit," she said firmly.

"You spoil my fun," the Major said with a mock pained expression on his face.

"Oh, I don't know about that," said Elizabeth walking up to him, embracing him and planting a great big juicy kiss on his lips. He put his arms around her and pulled her tight. They kissed again, maybe four or five times, or was it nine and ten. They wouldn't remember but suddenly had a sense of being watched. They stopped and turned and faced the shore. Sure enough, up by the railing on the road was a pair of Home Guard soldiers who had come to investigate the shadowy figures on the beach. As they stepped out of the water they became aware of another couple from the patrol who were at the top of the beach by the gardens on Queen Mary Road.

"Looks like it's time to beat a retreat," said the Major as he pulled his socks on.

"You got me into this situation. You get me out of it with my reputation intact," teased Elizabeth.

When they were both fully attired they made their way back through the anti-invasion barricade and up onto the path past the dragon's teeth on the slope and back onto Cliff Road. The two Home Guard soldiers by the railing turned to face them as the happy couple approached them. The Major said in a commanding voice,

"Been cleaning your rifle, soldier. Is that some flannelette I see in the butt of your gun?" The Home Guard swung his rifle off his shoulder and took a closer look at the end. By the time he realised he had been duped the Major and Elizabeth were past the soldiers without either of them now daring to say anything to such a senior officer. When they got to a safe distance where they couldn't be heard Elizabeth dissolved into a fit of giggles.

"Always works, that one. That's why I'm an officer and they are just troopers," said the Major in a self-satisfied tone. They slipped back into the hotel, climbed the stairs and said a passionate goodnight at the top of them before heading in separate directions to their rooms. They were both soon in bed and sleeping soundly. It was the first night for a while where there was no air raid siren to disrupt the sleep of the inhabitants of Falmouth.

Chapter Nineteen

The roses in Gyllyngdune Gardens were in full bloom and gave a wonderful fragrance as the last drops of dew evaporated from their petals. The Major and Elizabeth strolled slowly through as they took a Sunday morning walk having been fortified for the day by some Scots porridge served with a dollop of home made jam. A sailor and his girl were sat on the empty bandstand. The Major and Elizabeth passed by and headed down onto Melville Road. They were delighted just to be in each other's presence, to dawdle, to comment on this and that as they passed by and to hold the other's hand.

As they made their way along Western Terrace morning worshippers were heading to Emmanuel Church and they smiled at one dear lady's hat that looked as if she'd done some flower arranging in a chicken coup as blooms and feathers pointed out at all angles. They turned right and walked down Albany Place and continued into Lister Street, the most bombed street in Falmouth where a number of civilians had lost their lives. As they passed the empty shell where No 30 had stood until last July when it took a direct hit and killed five members of the same family their conversation turned to the war and when it was likely to end.

"The German attack against Russia means that the threat of invasion has passed for the time being because Hitler won't want to repeat the mistake of the last war and fight a land war on two fronts," said the Major.

"So that means we are less likely to lose but when will we be strong enough to rid Europe of the Nazi menace?" asked Elizabeth.

"When Churchill succeeds in getting the Americans into the war on our side," replied the Major.

"Is that what he's trying to do?" asked Elizabeth wondering how realistic a prospect that was. The United States was still officially neutral although their President had done what he could to help his country become the arsenal of the democracies.

"Most definitely," said the Major. "It's been the most important plank of government policy after sheer survival. Our government is already beginning planning on the invasion of Europe. Churchill is determined to win this war even if it takes several more years. He really feels the future of civilisation hangs on the Nazis being defeated and banished from the face of the earth."

"No more news from Vienna?" asked Elizabeth in a question that personalised the global conflict.

"Nothing," replied the Major with a tinge of sadness in his voice. The couple were now heading down Killigrew Street and soon passed the cinema where they had enjoyed their last visit to the town. They went to head out onto the Prince of Wales Pier but the gate was shut as a barrage balloon crew occupied the pier, so they strolled along Market Street looking at the shop windows selecting which fashions they liked, which furniture they would have in a home and then with a greater degree of difficulty which they thought the other liked. They pressed their noses on the glass at John Knights', at J.H. Lake's, at H Cox and Horder, at Robinsons and then as they passed on into Church Street at John Julians'. It was a young couple discovering each other's likes and dislikes, tastes and preferences. Eventually they emerged past Taylor's Garage and got a glimpse of the inner harbour and the submarine pier. They paused by the Killigrew Monument just as a naval officer was reading the inscription. He suddenly turned looked at the Major and said,

"Trevennel, is that really you? Good grief, man, it is!"

"Marshall," replied the Major with a look of delight on his face. "You still here in Falmouth? But you're going to have to tell me your rank, I can never keep up with all those rings."

"I'm a Paymaster Lieutenant Commander," replied Marshall. "Basically I'm a secretary to Flag Officer In Charge Falmouth."

"You're on Vice Admiral Kitson's staff," said the Major showing he wasn't entirely ignorant of the local naval chain of command.

"You've got it, my boy! So what are you doing? Army, obviously, but I don't recognise your insignia and you've no shoulder flashes," said Marshall returning the line of questioning.

"Military Intelligence is all I can say," replied the Major. "Oh do excuse me. Elizabeth, may I introduce Stephen Marshall who had the dubious privilege of sitting next to me in most of my classes at Falmouth Grammar School. Marshall," the Major reverted to the Grammar School tradition of referring to everyone by their surname, "May I introduce you to Corporal Elizabeth Treluckey."

"Very pleased to make your acquaintance," said Marshall with a smile as he inwardly congratulated his old school pal on having such a stunning beauty on his arm.

"So what brings you back home?" asked Marshall.

"This is a weekend of indulgent pleasure," said the Major glancing at Elizabeth, "But I'm in Cornwall on business," he added but revealing no more of the work that he was engaged in. "What are you up to? How's the war going in HMS Forte?" asked the Major using the Falmouth shore base name.

"Been busy compiling reports for a Board of Inquiry we've got tomorrow. In fact, it's the second one we've had on this particular ship," said Marshall revealing a little more than he probably should have.

"Well, let's meet up for a drink tomorrow evening," said the Major. "Give you something to look forward tomorrow as you sit through all those tedious questions."

"Splendid idea. Where?"

"I'm staying at the Pentargon. Come and find me there," said the Major. The arrangement was sealed with a handshake and the old friends parted company.

"I probably haven't seen him since the start of the war," said the Major to Elizabeth as they strode along Bar Road. "Funny how life turns out. Marshall was always intent on a career in the navy following in both his father's and grandfather's footsteps. He used to try and persuade me to join the Senior Service when we were at school but it was always the army for me."

"Well, you both seem to have done alright out of the choices you made," said Elizabeth. "Now we need to step it up if we are to make lunch back at the hotel."

The couple dined well and then walked out again, this time heading across Berkeley Vale to Trevethan Road where Elizabeth was keen to attend the afternoon service in the Gospel Hall. The evening service had been brought forward earlier in the war as a result of the black out and the air raids. It was a church known to Elizabeth as it was where her parents had married just after the Great War and where Elizabeth had attended as a young child before the move to the Camel Estuary when an aunt left them the small farm. The family had enjoyed the fellowship whenever they had stayed with relatives in the town on several occasions before the war.

Thus as they approached the entrance they were greeted warmly by John Stych who recognised Elizabeth despite her being in uniform. Once inside the Major was introduced to Elizabeth's maternal grandparents and several other relatives. After the excitement had abated everyone took their seats and the service began. It was a novel experience for the Major whose only sampling of this style of Christian worship had been when he had gate-crashed the end of a similar meeting whilst trying to track down Elizabeth's father last summer. That had turned out well for him, he thought as he sat gazing around at the square meeting room, so hopefully this one will bring some good dividend.

A man dressed in a suit rather than any kind of religious robe or regalia led the first part of the service with various hymns, a prayer and an account of how God had helped him during the difficult years of the Thirties depression. He then handed over to a naval officer in uniform who read from the Bible and spoke about Jesus fulfilling the prophecy of Isaiah chapter sixty one in proclaiming the year of the Lord's favour. He said the proclamation of the day of God's vengeance would occur when Jesus returns to earth again. He then turned to the New Testament and read from Luke chapter four where Jesus in the synagogue quoted the Jewish prophet but stopped in the middle of the saying after the words "to proclaim the year of the Lord's favour." It was new and fascinating to the Major and his mind drifted to the challenge Elizabeth had set him that night in the bedroom at his parent's house to read the Gospel accounts for himself. He had not done so. He knew he had been busy but he resolved to himself he would have to get round to doing so. The service concluded with another hymn and a prayer.

The couple must have had four invites to tea at the end of the service but Elizabeth elected to go home with her grandparents. The Major sensed they pulled rank in the family hierarchy, but several of the other members of the family seemed to join them after dashing home to bring and share their own teatime provisions. The grandparents lived in a house on Tregothnan Road, just a short distance away. They apologised that the front garden looked a mess but they were still getting straight from the bombs that had fallen on neighbouring roads in February and blown all their windows out and brought some of the roof slates down. They said they couldn't complain as a retired bank manager and two women had lost their lives in the raid that had also dropped the mine in the harbour that had killed the team of divers when it exploded a couple of weeks later.

The Major was taken with the friendly and welcoming family and felt at home amidst the happy occasion. Fortunately he was not plied with too many questions about his war service. The family were keen to hear all the ins and outs of Elizabeth's life in the ATS. He was surprised at how the time had flown when Elizabeth finally suggested they took their leave. There were hugs and kisses all round and the grandparents made the Major promise he would call in if he was at a loose end in Falmouth even if Elizabeth wasn't with him.

It was a slow and lingering walk back to the hotel on the sea front, neither wanting their wonderful time together to come to an end. They stood by the railing above Castle Beach watching the waves lap against the rocks for a while before heading indoors. It was another peaceful night's sleep before the Major walked Elizabeth down to the station to catch the early morning train to Truro and her connection up the main line.

"Thank you so much for a wonderful time," said Elizabeth leaning out of the carriage window for yet another goodbye kiss.

"I'll be in touch as soon as work allows," promised the Major. He stood and waved until the train had completely disappeared out of sight up the branch line. He then walked back to the hotel to pick up the car and drive down to Housel Bay for that day's inspection of the security arrangements at the new radar station at Pen Olver. He was glad he was busy. It would take his mind off missing Elizabeth too much.

Chapter Twenty

There were only a couple of people having drinks in the lounge bar of the Pentargon that evening when the Major stepped in. He was surprised to find his old friend Marshall already there, sat with a drink glass held between his two hands slowly swirling the drink round and round. He went up to him and said,

"Penny for them." It made his old friend jump. His mind was obviously elsewhere.

"Oh, er, hello. Good to see you," he stammered. Then as he recovered, "What are you drinking? This one's on me." When the two men had their drinks the Major suggested they move next door to the deserted drawing room where they found comfy chairs either side of the fireplace.

The first salvos of the conversation were all about catching up. Marshall wanted to know how the Major had met Elizabeth and how serious the relationship was. The Major left him in no doubt that there was not the slightest hope of poaching the ATS corporal from him. After catching up on the news of a number of their old classmates the conversation turned to the Board Of Inquiry that the naval officer had attended today. He was reluctant to speak of it, obviously under oath of secrecy, but the Major sensed he was a man carrying a burden. The Major pulled out a letter from the inside pocket of his tunic and gave it to Marshall. It was one he had used many times to show that he had the highest security clearance and requested that the reader offer all possible assistance to the Major in the pursuit of his duties.

"Wow! Firing with the big guns," said Marshall as he handed the letter back.

"You look like you could do with being able to offload a burden to a friendly listening ear that is not directly involved in the matters you are dealing with," said the Major with a genuine concern for his friend. "It goes no further," he added as he put his glass down on the small table between them.

"There was a major incident on board a ship off the Cornish coast at the end of May. Today was the second Board of Inquiry we have held into the conduct on that fateful night. My job has been to compile all the witness statements prior to the sittings. I've even had to travel to Wales to interview one sailor recovering in hospital, and today I was overseeing the shorthand secretaries that were recording the day's proceedings. Some of the actions of Admiralty leave a lot to be desired. FOIC Falmouth has tried to raise one or two concerns but he has been sat on by those higher up, and whereas one would normally say to oneself 'They probably have a more complete picture than I do' and let it go, I am confident in this case they don't but I am at a loss as to what one can do." There was an earnestness about the young naval officer, who took a sip of his drink as he paused.

"You can start at the beginning," said the Major leaning back in his chair and making himself comfortable for a long evening. Marshall took a deep breath and started.

“HMS Registan was a steam merchant vessel of just over six thousand tons laid down in 1930 in the South Shields for Strick & Co. of London. She was requisitioned for the navy in September 1940 and converted into an Ocean Boarding Vessel. Her role was enforcing wartime blockades by intercepting and boarding foreign vessels. However on 24th May she left the Clyde heading for Southampton carrying 1319 tons of general cargo.”

“General cargo? Would that have included ammunition or other dangerous items?” asked the Major.

“Possibly, there are accounts of her carrying empty drums, but as she was armed there would have been ammunition on board,” said Marshall. “It was not unusual for Registan to support convoys in home waters and she would be used to carry whatever was necessary.”

“What armament did she have?” asked the Major.

“She was classed as an Armed Merchant Vessel and was provided with one three inch gun and two Hotchkiss aft, two Hotchkiss on the bridge and some Holman Projectors amidships.” The naval officer reeled off the detail showing he was obviously very familiar with every facet of the vessel as it and its crew had occupied every waking hour of his life for the last month.

“All was proceeding well until the Commander in Chief Plymouth sent an order at 0956 on the 26th May to proceed to Milford Haven. Although naval logs show this was transmitted by Land's End from 1034 on the 26th it was not received by the ship until 0230 on the 27th."

"Why the delay?" asked the Major.

"The Captain said he had no wavelengths to be monitored in his sailing directions. He claimed he was told by the Senior Rating at Greenock that six hundred metres was the wavelength he should keep on a coastal passage. So he did. The signal was sent on 107 metres. The radio officer just happened to switch his second receiver on to 107 metres just after 0200 and by chance heard the message for his ship."

"So which was the correct wavelength? Who was at fault?" asked the Major.

"The regulations do not mention Ocean Boarding Vessels. As an Armed Merchant Vessel she should have been given clear instructions. The departure signal on the 24th failed to do so. The ship did what it could with limited manpower to keep watch on the known channels as best she could according to the available regulations." The naval officer knew his answer implied criticism of Admiralty colleagues at Greenock.

"So where was the ship when it finally received the message to change course?" asked the Major.

"It had already rounded Land's End and was proceeding along the south Cornish coast," said Marshall.

"What did the Captain do?"

"Obeyed orders. He turned Registan and went back round Land's End."

“But that’s dangerous water,” said the Major. “Not just because of the currents. The threat from U-boats or aircraft is extremely high.”

“Agreed. When the ship hadn’t made Milford Haven the Commander in Chief Plymouth sent a message at 0150 on the 27th asking the Captain to report his position at 0600 on the 27th. The message was despatched at 0237. Registan responded at 0306 saying the messages had been received and she was proceeding to Milford Haven with an ETA of 1600 that day. She gave what her position would be at 0600 which was just north west of Cape Cornwall. That means she had probably been as far along the coast as Falmouth Bay when she was ordered to turn round.” The naval officer paused and took a sip of his drink.

“So what time did she finally make Milford Haven?” asked the Major.

“She didn’t. By early afternoon she was logged by Hartland Point Coastguard Station at 1432 heading across the Bristol Channel towards Milford Haven when she received a message saying ‘Cancel my order of 0956/26. Proceed in execution of previous orders.’ The order had been sent at 0656 but wasn’t received on board until 1430. So the Captain turned his ship once more and was logged by Hartland Point Coastguards at 1549 heading back down the coast towards Land’s End.”

“What I don’t understand,” said the Major honestly, “Is why the delay between orders being sent and received? The navy is meticulous in its procedures.”

"The Chief gives the order. It's typed, encoded and sent to the wireless room at Mount Wise. They send it to the appropriate transmitting stations around the coast. In this case Land's End. They transmit it on pre-agreed wavelengths. When it's picked up by the ship it's written down, decoded and then passed to the bridge."

"But this is often done in minutes," said a puzzled Major.

"What else was happening that day?" asked Marshall. "May 27th." The Major paused and racked his brains. Then it hit him.

"Bismarck," he exclaimed.

"Exactly. The hunt was on for the Bismarck and by that time they were closing for the kill. All wireless traffic relating to that would have been marked 'Priority' and everything else would be left in the ever growing pile to be transmitted when the operatives had chance to catch up." Marshall picked up his glass and sat back in his chair and downed the last mouthful. The Major began putting the pieces of the jigsaw together.

"So Registan is further round the coast than Plymouth think when it's told to change course and go for Milford Haven. So the Captain sails round Land's End with all its inherent dangers for the second time. Admiralty then catch up, realise where she was and cancel the order, but because of the delay she's already off North Devon. So she's now got to go round Land's End again but presumably this time in daylight."

"Exactly. Coastal vessels in daylight are provided with air escort. So as she sails down the North Cornish coast there are Spitfires from 66 Squadron at Portreath patrolling over the shipping lanes. There's been a lot of air activity off Cornwall and in the Western Approaches that evening. Radar plots show that about ninety German aircraft were sent to attack shipping."

"To revenge the sinking of the Bismarck," said the Major as he sensed the story was about to get a whole lot worse. He stood up. "Let me get you another drink from the bar." Marshall gave his order and the Major headed out the door. The naval officer sighed. It was good to talk and share the burden with a friend. Usually in this war there was never chance to do that. Friends were worth having.

Chapter Twenty One

Johann made his way back to his lodgings having spent his evening in the King's Hotel. The food had been good, the beer was passable but the conversations he had overheard had been most interesting. He was encouraged to learn that the German advance against Soviet Russia was progressing well. It seems Stalin's forces were struggling to cope with the speed of the Panzer columns. British Prime Minister Churchill had promised all possible help but Johann doubted that would ever amount to much. He learned that the Canadian Prime Minister was in London. He also heard that the pilot of the German plane that crashed into the sea near the Manacles was alive although it seemed several of his crew had drowned.

At the dockyard he had stirred up a few of the workers who were unhappy about the fire-watching duties they were expected to do on top of their long shifts, especially at the weekend. Johann had urged them not to carry them out unless the management paid them for the task. He had told the disgruntled men that they wouldn't find the managers on the roof tops during an air raid. It was the first example of industrial unrest he had come across and he did what he could to stoke the anger.

Johann had also volunteered for a work party who were due to be taken tomorrow to a vessel that was beached near St Mawes. They were tasked with removing ammunition from the burned out vessel that had been towed in by the tug Goliath several weeks ago. He thought it would be a good opportunity to cross the harbour and have a look at its defences on the far shore as well as having a closer look at the shipping moored in the Carrick Roads.

The only concern of the evening was when two Dutch Naval officer cadets from their training college at Enys House near Penryn came into the hotel and bought drinks at the bar. Johann decided that was the time to call it a day just in case anyone recognised him and wanted to introduce him to the Dutchmen and so finished his pint and headed back through the streets to his room in Bar Road. He let himself in and stretched out on his bed to read the newspaper he had picked up after its owner had left it on a table in the hotel.

Elizabeth waited for the sentry to lift the barrier at the West Gate of the barracks. It had been an unexpected trip but she was satisfied with her errand of mercy. A party of Land Army girls had broken down in their truck on the way back from a farm near Helland and a phone call had come into the barracks to rescue the young women and take them back to their hostel in Barn Lane. Elizabeth had volunteered to go herself instead of delegating the task to one of the girls. She thought it was a good way to stay in Sergeant Buscombe's good books so that she might look kindly on her when she wanted a pass to be able to spend time with the Major.

Elizabeth eventually found the party of six sat on the back of their truck singing at the top of their voices to pass the time until they were rescued. Elizabeth's arrival was greeted with a great cheer. They felt their truck had burned out its clutch on a hill near Lecudden. One of the party had had to walk to the next farm at Penhargard to find a phone with which to summon help.

A tow truck wouldn't be available until morning, so the matron of the Land Army hostel had appealed to the ATS to rescue her girls and save them being stuck on the farm all night.

Two of the girls sat in the cab with Elizabeth and the other four stood in the back. Elizabeth instantly recognised the smells of a day working on a farm and it made her think of home. She wondered how her parents and her younger brother were doing. It had been some time since she had last been home. Elizabeth had only just pulled away and the girls struck up again.

"*If you want to go to Heaven when you die,*
Wear a pair of khaki breeches and an old felt bonnet,
Join the W.L.A. and sing this sonnet,
If you want to go to Heaven when you die."

The singing turned a few heads as they came down Berry Lane and into Pool Street. A couple of soldiers stood outside the White Hart public house jeered and waved as the girls passed. Elizabeth drove up Crockwell Street and turned right up Fore Street. It was only as the hostel came into view in Barn Lane that the singing died down. Elizabeth pulled up in front of the newly built concrete block building. The hostel matron came out and invited Elizabeth in to join them for supper as a thank you for collecting her girls. Elizabeth politely declined the kind offer and wished them all well. She then drove over the Beacon and down the hill, over the railway and was at the gate of the Depot. She reported 'Mission accomplished' to Sergeant Buscombe and then turned in for an early night.

Chapter Twenty Two

"The ship was eight miles off Cape Cornwall heading round Land's End for the third time when the attack came," said Paymaster Lieutenant Commander Marshall continuing his tale to his old school friend Major Isaac Trevennel. "Daylight was fast fading as it passed ten o'clock. The escort, a Blenheim fighter bomber and two Spitfires, had just left so they could land without their airfield needing to illuminate the runway lights. The ship was at action stations. It had been put into two watches for coming round the coast.

"The first anyone saw of the German planes were two greeny grey aircraft closing from 1500 yards head on just fifty feet above the water. The bridge was raked by machine gun fire and the planes flew just over the top of the mast. A bomb hit the aft deck. The Hotchkiss on the bridge fired but the planes were too low for the three inch anti-aircraft gun to fire.

"The Captain investigated the damage and was told the engine room was leaking and the dynamo was in danger of being flooded. There was also an unexploded 250 lb bomb on the aft deck lying at the bottom of the starboard poop ladder. A collision mat was sent with the care and maintenance party to deal with the hole in the engine room thought to be caused by the explosion of a near miss. There were several incendiary bombs across the after deck but these were dealt with by the crew, some armed with fire extinguishers. A team of five tried moving the unexploded bomb but couldn't lift it so used a sling from the depth charge thrower davit and had just hoisted it up when the second attack came from the stern fifteen minutes after the first.

"Three planes came in their machine guns blazing and dropped high explosive and incendiary bombs. One plane dropped a bomb on or very close to the funnel, two bombs struck around the engine room, one of which went in the stokehold, and a third on the after deck. The engines stopped and smoke and steam rose from the engine room and the whole place came alight. Incendiary bombs caught the bridge house alight. The galley tank on the boat deck was torn open and over two hundred tons of fuel oil was sprayed all over the deck and made the fire worse. The steam pipes had burst and there was no water to fight the fires except for the fire extinguishers which the crew used but were totally inadequate against the conflagration.

"The three inch gun had fired about four rounds until it was put out of action. The two Hotchkiss guns aft fired until put out of action. Those on the bridge had to be abandoned because of the fire burning the wooden deck beneath them. The Holman Projectors were put out of action when the funnel fell on them. Electric power was lost during this second attack and the lights went out. Within a couple of minutes the whole of amidships was ablaze. The Captain gave the order to abandon the bridge and some of the crew began to assemble on the fore well deck. There were a good number of casualties by this time and several of the crew have described helping the wounded or stopping to tend to their needs and carry them away from the fires." Marshall paused to take a sip of his drink. The Major sat in silence struggling to comprehend the horrors that must have unfolded before the crew that night. Marshall continued,

"In the third attack the ship was again raked with machine gun fire and bombs were dropped amidships and one on the after deck by number three hatch. One of the aft Hotchkiss gunners tried returning to his gun but it wouldn't fire and he was then hit by a bullet in the mouth. There were crew on the foredeck, a smaller number on the aft deck, amidships was well ablaze and the ship began to list.

"The two starboard lifeboats had been destroyed, the port cutter was useless because the steel winch had been thrown about ten feet from its base and the steel falls were jammed. The Captain then asked for volunteers to try and make it through the fire to the aft lifeboat to see if that could be used. Six volunteered. Incredibly three officers succeeded and found the lifeboat intact. They cut the falls of the steel lifeboat and it fell into the water fortunately landing the right way up. They took the wounded from the aft deck into the lifeboat and then having hauled several men out of the water, some of whom had jumped to escape the fire, made forward to evacuate the wounded from the foredeck. They had lowered a number of wounded into the lifeboat when one of the planes came over again and the lifeboat was hit by machine gun fire. It began taking water. They continued loading the wounded and were strafed again. One bomb exploded in the water just five yards from the lifeboat.

"The Captain was concerned the lifeboat was being targeted and would be lost so as the plane came in again ordered the lifeboat to lay off until it was quiet again. At some point two

Spitfires returning from patrol saw the fire from off Trevose Head near Padstow and arrived between the second and third attacks and dispersed the planes but the German aircraft kept coming back and strafing the ship when they had opportunity to do so. One of the planes a Heinkel 111 was shot down and crashed into the sea off Gurnard's Head killing all the crew. Another was damaged and seen with its wheels down. This Heinkel 111 was chased from St Ives to Mousehole where it glided to a halt on the sea. The plane was observed to sink but the crew were rescued by a German boat from the Seenotdienst. The planes had also been attacking shore targets as a bomb was dropped in Newlyn harbour and a young Home Guard lad died from his wounds and several others wounded when the port was machine gunned.

"The German planes continued to make strafing runs on the Registan and the lifeboat which showed up in the glare of the burning ship. So eventually the lifeboat made for the shore eight miles away.

"The remaining ship's crew managed to get some Carley Floats into the water although some of these were hit in the machine gun fire and bombing. On board the Captain gave the order that rafts be made from the timber stored for damage control and this was done. The ship lurched and the Captain gave the order to abandon ship and a number of men went over the side. When the ship listed no further he cancelled the order. Those in the water made for the two surviving Carley floats or had lifebuoys. The Carley Floats were cut adrift from the ship as they were full. A couple of men who had gone into the water to help the wounded into the floats managed to climb the ropes and get back on board the ship and reported the water was cold. Further rafts were made and a count made of the men remaining on the ship. There were nineteen. When a little while later the ship gave another lurch and was now listing severely the Captain again ordered “Abandon ship!” The last wounded man on the foredeck was strapped to a raft and lowered into the water. The men went over the side and were clinging to the rafts and pieces of timber which had been thrown into the water. The German planes continued to machine gun the men in the water.

“Eventually the planes left and the men began to drift away from the burning ship. Two men decided to swim back to the ship and take their chances on board. They were still there when HMS Wyvern, HMS Wild Swan and HMS Vansittart who had been dispatched from Plymouth just after 2300 hours arrived on the scene in the small hours of the morning. Wyvern approached the ship and its whaler took the two men off the burning hulk just before 0330. Wild Swan found one of the Carley Floats about 0400 and rescued the seventeen exhausted men. They also found four men in the water clinging to bits of wood and rescued them. Four of those the Wild Swan rescued never regained consciousness and died. Vansittart picked up four seamen who were already dead and rescued nineteen clinging to flotsam including the Captain.”

“What happened to the second Carley Float?” asked the Major.

“This was the starboard side float. The bombing and the tide brought it round the bow of the boat where it had several near misses from bombs and the strafing. The men tried to paddle but there were only a couple with the strength to do so as many were wounded. They drifted in the current until they were found by the fishing boat Ruby which had put out from Sennen Cove manned by five of the lifeboat crew under the Second Coxswain as the lifeboat was unable to launch as it was being overhauled. There were just four left alive in the float when rescued, one of whom was seriously wounded. When the Ruby attempted to use a Morse signal lamp they were machine gunned. They landed back at Sennen at 0315. The St Ives lifeboat was launched but didn't rescue anyone."

"And the ship's lifeboat?"

"It was spotted at seven the following morning by a Spitfire off the north Cornish coast. It was eventually beached in a small cove off Gurnard's Head. One of the officers climbed the cliff to raise the alarm but the Spitfire pilot had already dropped a message in his gauntlet to the nearest farm to give assistance. The survivors were helped up the cliff by locals, the Coastguard and an ambulance and a bus were used to ferry them to hospital in Penzance."

"What happened to the other survivors?" enquired the Major.

"As a couple of motor launches and the tug Goliath arrived on the scene just before dawn the three warships were ordered to take their survivors to Milford Haven. However the Captain of the Wyvern had decided that as the fire appeared to be burning itself out, it would be possible to place some men back on board, so he sent an order to the Vansittart to get the Captain of the Registan to get a party to go back to their ship. The Captain and five others went and stayed on board as the vessel was eventually towed back into Falmouth still burning. When the fire was eventually extinguished on the 29th May a large unexploded bomb was found on board. We've managed to find the charred remains of over twenty bodies on board and they've been buried in the cemetery here in Falmouth.

"And the total number of casualties?" asked the sombre Major.

"Sixty eight dead or missing presumed dead, fifty four survivors." Having reached the end of his account Marshall appeared drained and emotionally exhausted.

"It's remarkable from what you have described that so many survived," said the Major. "No doubt through acts of courage and bravery, such as going through the fire to get the lifeboat released."

"The reason for the second inquiry was an allegation from one of the wounded that the officers merely acted for themselves. But we have found there was no cowardice, no panic, and incredible acts of bravery. Those that made it through the fire to get the lifeboat did so by climbing on the stanchions and handrails which they said were burning hot. Having got aft there was no way back so their only recourse was to bring the lifeboat forward in the water.

"When the Captain ordered the bridge to be abandoned except for the two Hotchkiss gunners, he stayed with them until the wooden deck was burning away beneath their feet and then he ordered them down and he was the last to leave. They had to come down the Sampson post in order to escape. There were attempts to rescue those caught in the fire until they were beaten back by the flames."

"And this is the bravery of our sailors and merchant seamen that is happening every day to win the Battle of the Atlantic," said the Major.

"Yes, we lost a Norwegian merchant vessel that same evening in Bude Bay to attack by aircraft. But this one was avoidable. Because all eyes were on the Bismarck the Registan suffered this fate."

"The sinking of the Bismarck was vital. She could have created havoc among the convoys," said the Major. "It was right she was the priority."

"That I understand," said Marshall. "But try telling that to the families of those who have perished, especially those lost at sea. All they will have is a place and a name. If only she had been left to continue on her course. To be made to sail round Land's End three times is absolute folly. But Admiralty shrugs its shoulders and carries on. No one is accountable. The families will never be told what I've told you. It will be just more lives lost in the fog of war."

"In all wars mistakes are made, but it's pressing on towards victory that is the key. That's what those who have paid the ultimate sacrifice would have wanted. Everyone was doing their best with what they had to do what they could at the time. We can't ask for any more, not even of Admiralty. History will judge us on whether we were right."

"Are lives so cheap?" asked Marshall with a distant look in his eyes revealing he was haunted by the unnecessary loss of so many of the crew of HMS Registan.

"Never," said the Major with a fierce determination. "The peace that we will win will be paid for in the deaths of men like those in the Registan and, I fear, in a good many more ships and planes and battlefields yet. That peace, when we win it, we need to treasure and to protect. Freedom is not free. We must appreciate the cost and teach that to our children. We allowed Hitler to snatch peace away from Europe so quickly after the Great War. We must not allow anyone to do that again."

"With that I agree. I guess I have been so focused on the minute detail for the last month I am in danger of losing the bigger picture," said Marshall in an honest assessment of his thinking.

"We can all do that so easily," said the Major. "Defeating Hitler is the goal. Let's get a refill and drink to the brave men and women who are doing just that. Fortify yourself, Marshall. There'll be another battle to fight tomorrow." With his old school friend's stirring words ringing in his ears he followed the Major out to the bar for another drink and the determination to win the war for the sake of those whose lives it had claimed.

Chapter Twenty Three

The Major's tour of military installations continued through the week. He had spent a couple of hours with Major Christie at the Gun Operations Room at Penhale House on the Trelissick Estate at Feock. From here all the anti-aircraft guns that defended Falmouth were controlled. He was shown the plotting table with its huge map of the west of Cornwall. There were a bank of telephones that carried direct lines to the six heavy gun sites around Falmouth, to a further five across west Cornwall from Buller Down to Raginnis and Trevedra. There was also a hotline to HMS Forte, lines to Pendennis Castle, St Mawes Castle and St Antony Fort and lines to 959 Squadron of the RAF that manned Falmouth's balloon barrage.

Major Christie felt the site was that far up the Carrick Roads that they were not at risk of an enemy incursion unless there was a full scale invasion. When the Major informed him two dead Germans had been discovered last summer in a rubber dinghy on the creek less than a mile from where they were stood, he began to take the Major's comments a little more seriously.

When the Major left the GOR he turned right down the hill and went across the King Harry Ferry onto the Roseland peninsula. The deep river Fal looked a beautiful blue on this quiet summer's day and they edged from one bank to the other. The steep sides of the ria covered in woodland made it an enchanting place. It brought back childhood memories of the day his father had taken him and his brother by boat up the river and the picnic they had in the park on the riverbank at

Truro before using the outgoing tide to race back down the estuary. As he drove up the hill from the ferry his mind turned to wondering where his brother was now. Was he free? Was he in hiding with the rest of the family? Would the American press agency be able to assist them in any way? Or were they in the clutches of the Nazis? All he could do was to help defeat Hitler and his way of doing that right now was inspecting the security arrangements of yet another establishment.

He drove down the narrow lane towards Porthcurnick Beach but before reaching the sand pulled right into the grounds of a large Victorian house. There was no sentry at the gate. The Major pulled up in front of the house, got out and knocked on the front door. A naval rating answered the door and when the Major introduced himself welcomed him in.

Porthcurnick House was an outpost of HMS Forte. It was an ASDIC Station. They had a variety of hydrophonic equipment to be able to try and detect the movement of enemy submarines in the water. A number of cables ran out of what had originally been the front room of the house and down to the beach and from there out to sea. This is where they put the experimental work the Major had seen at Perranporth into practice as part of the defence of Falmouth.

The small outpost had experienced tragedy just before Christmas. One of its ratings had discovered an enemy mine washed up on the beach at a time when the navy were very concerned about the new acoustic and magnetic mines the Germans were using. He carried it up to the house and proceeded to dismantle it. It exploded and he was killed and buried in the churchyard at nearby Gerrans.

The Major was told the main security was secrecy as to what actually went on in the house. As with all naval outposts there were clear instructions on what to destroy in the event of the ship being overrun. The beach was protected by scaffolding that ran right across it. Whilst there were no pillboxes here or at Porthscatho the Home Guard used the old boatman's shelter by the slipway at Porthscatho as a lookout and there were pillboxes on the neighbouring beaches of Towan, Pendower and Carne and at Creek Stephen Point. The naval rating assured the Major they felt quite safe and said they had a daily wireless contact with HMS Forte in Falmouth so were kept abreast of naval communications in the event of any emergency. The Major wished them well and took his leave.

Elizabeth ran her hands through her hair. She was exasperated. The lecture had already lasted almost an hour and she was struggling to tell the difference between a Junkers 86 and a Junkers 89 let alone a Heinkel 111 and a Dornier 17. She had seen enough of the poster on the board at the front of the hall with its various silhouettes. She was ready for lunch. 'I bet the Major would get them all right in any test,' she thought as her mind wandered onto more interesting topics. She wondered where in the county he was visiting today and when she might get chance to see him again. She was on duty all this coming weekend so there was no hope then. However, she was hopeful for the following weekend but would the Major still be here or would he be back in London. The thought of a visit to the capital was attractive to Elizabeth. She had never been there. In fact, she hadn't ventured further than Plymouth, but she would have to wait for a seven day leave before even attempting a visit. If she tried it on a weekend pass she could spend the whole 48 hours just travelling there and back. But the prospects of a week off were very slim. Still the hope of another weekend with the Major in Cornwall would keep her going this week. The question startled her and jolted her from her musings.

"How many crew in a Heinkel 111?" asked DCLI Sergeant Fox.

"Four, sir," said Elizabeth guessing as she'd gleaned that most German bombers they'd covered during the morning seemed to have a crew of either three or four.

"Correct, corporal. I thought we'd lost you there for a moment, but you obviously were paying attention," said the sergeant. "Well, I hope that's taught you girls enough that you won't embarrass yourselves when you visit the Royal Observer Corps this afternoon. That concludes my talk. Class dismissed."

Elizabeth enjoyed the soup and hunk of bread they were given for lunch. It was vegetable but potato and carrot appeared to be the predominant ingredients. Half an hour later she brought the truck onto the parade ground and the ATS girls that had made up the aircraft recognition class this morning duly piled into the back. It was only a short drive up onto the Beacon but they bumped and jolted along once Elizabeth left the tarmac road at the top of the hill and cut up the Beacon Lane. She headed for the Gilbert Obelisk and pulled up on the grass next to it.

There to meet them were two members of the Royal Observer Corps. Very proud that in April they were designated 'Royal', they introduced themselves as Observer Ellis, who was better known as the local press photographer, and Observer Standfield, who was an electrician in civilian life. They showed the ATS girls around their two storey post built just in front of the hedge surrounding the Beacon and explained how they worked in a triangle with posts at Par and St Breward all reporting to the Control Centre in Truro. They taught the girls to use the post instrument to plot an aircraft and two of them got to do it for real when two Spitfires returning from a south coast patrol passed over heading back towards their north coast aerodrome. The men checked the plot and then phoned the details through to Truro. They explained usually one man did the observing while the other did the talking and that way the Control Centre could be kept up to date with where the aircraft was. This had proved so vital during the Battle of Britain that it earned them their 'Royal' designation from His Majesty King George VI. The girls tried testing the two observers on their aircraft recognition by framing questions from what they had been taught that morning. They were very impressed that the two men could answer every detail requested of them. They thanked the men for their time, left them to continue their duty and piled back into the truck for the ride down the hill.

The tug made its way slowly through the shipping lying at anchor in the harbour and headed across the water towards St Mawes. The work party from the docks under the control of a chargehand were being transported to where a bombed and burned out ship was beached. Johann was delighted to be among their number. He was stood at the tug's rail for the journey so he could observe as much of the shipping as possible and get a better idea of what kind of vessels were moored either awaiting orders or awaiting their slot in the dockyard for repair. However, when they were only halfway across his attention was drawn towards St Mawes Castle. Not that he was particularly interested in the fort built in the time of Henry VIII as part of England's defence against the threat of invasion, but he had spotted a well camouflaged searchlight battery built on the water's edge just below the walls of the castle. He counted four searchlights and wondered how visible they would be from the air. He surmised they'd be obvious once they had exposed their light but these were part of the harbour defence designed to illuminate attacking boats. The four buildings were not weather worn and had not been lashed by the sea so they had to be new.

He then made out some construction work going on to the north of the castle. As they got closer he could see that it was a gun battery that was being built. There was no sign of a gun yet so he couldn't say what calibre, but it was obvious the harbour's defences were being strengthened. They seemed to be constructing some sort of tower as part of the gun emplacement. He would have to keep an eye on its progress to see what developed. There was a nissen hut between the battery and the castle which he assumed would house the soldiers involved in the work.

The tug passed Castle Point and slowed as it came into St Mawes Bay. The hulk of the ship they had come to work on dominated the view. It was evident there had been a large fire amidships although the bow and stern seemed untouched. Moored just off her was the HMS Princess Victoria which in happier days had been used to take trippers sightseeing up and down the Fal. The master of the tug brought his vessel into the steamer and the men grabbed their haversacks and made up the rope ladder onto the aft deck of the ship. It was a scene of utter devastation. Items were strewn all over the deck which was holed in a number of places by explosion and machine gun fire.

There was a naval party aboard and an officer came and spoke to the chargehand. The naval party, along with an undertaker and his crew, were there to locate and remove the bodies of those who had perished on the ship. The lieutenant indicated they were working in the flooded stokehold. Johann's work party's orders were to remove the ammunition still on the ship. They would need to check all the ready use lockers and the holds. They were warned of deep voids where the fire had burned away all the woodwork but otherwise the metalwork had cooled sufficiently for them to access all the areas they needed to go.

The chargehand divided them into two teams of five men each. Johann was in the chargehand's group which would start at the bow. The other group were to start at the gun platform above the aft deck. Johann and his companions followed the chargehand forward. Where the wooden section of the ship once had stood they paused staggered by the evidence of the intensity of the fire. Here had stood the cabins that led up to the ward rooms and bridge. Here the metal was blackened except where it had been hit by the machine gun bullets which had gouged out silver indentations. The foredeck was strewn with pieces of timber and various possessions that the crew had obviously abandoned. A pair of shoes, an oilskin jacket, a bandage, ropes tied and dangling over the side of the ship, all left behind as the men had sought safety in the water.

They set to work and climbed below deck to start checking the holds. The party working on the stern started removing the ammunition from the ready locker of the three inch gun. The gun lay twisted having been hit by gunfire. From the amount they removed they concluded the gun had not fired many rounds. They began to pile the crates in a clear space on the aft deck ready to be taken onto the barge that the tug would return with when it came to pick them up. By the time they broke for lunch there was a sizeable collection. Both teams decided to eat their food on the fore deck as the naval party had laid several body bags containing the charred remains they had discovered during their morning's work on the aft deck.

It was only as they were tucking into their sandwiches that the conversation began to flow for the first time. Much of the morning there had been an absence of small talk, partly as they set to and partly as a reaction to the horror of the setting. As the men bemoaned their lot at the task Johann sought to stoke the resentment and stir the emotions of the men. When the men had caught the bait he then raised the issue of the items scattered over the deck and the possessions they'd seen still hanging in some of the cabins below deck.

"Who's going to have those now? The crew won't be coming back for them," he suggested. "I think you've earned the right to some extras today. A little bonus from Admiralty for the hard and difficult task you have been assigned to do." Some of the men were horrified at the suggestion of pilfering from the ship, although they knew it was rife across the dockyard. However, Johann knew he had planted the seed, especially with his team who had seen below decks much more than those working on the stern. As they returned to work he again dangled the prospect of helping themselves to items of use or interest.

At the end of the day when the tug returned on the tide, the men lowered the crates of ammunition down onto the barge and lashed it down for the journey back across the estuary. They then collected their haversacks and climbed down onto the tug. Johann noticed the naval officer watching them closely, but he said nothing. When he turned to talk to one of his men, the chargehand picked up a piano accordion from behind a bulwark and passed it down to one of the men in the tug. When the tug's master commented on it, one of Johann's team opened his rucksack and took out some tins of condensed milk and a tin of corned beef and gave them to the master. He gratefully accepted and stashed them out of sight before setting course for Falmouth.

The next day the men were back again continuing with the task. This time as they left one of the men passed the tug's master a pair of shoes. Another of Johann's team was wearing an oilskin coat that he'd not arrived at work with. Johann knew the chargehand had picked up the pair of binoculars Johann had spotted lying amongst the debris on the deck and pointed out to him.

The following day when Johann arrived at the docks there was an air of concern among the men of his team. Talking in hushed voices, they soon revealed to Johann that the tug's master had been questioned by the police. They agreed that they would take nothing that day and seek to hide the stolen items they had already procured. As they moved off towards the tug, Johann told the chargehand he needed to use the toilet and would catch them up by the time they reached the wharf. Johann was concerned. The last thing he needed was to become embroiled in a police investigation that might reveal his identity and endanger his mission. It was time to move on. He doubled back and caught up with the line of night shift workers who were exiting the dockyard. He would not go and work on HMS Registan today. He would head instead to the last target on his mission and then would seek out his escape route. He removed his work ticket and put it in his pocket, ducked back out the same door and joined the stream of men heading for home. Once outside the dock he ripped his ticket up and dropped it in the dustbin of the first house in Bar Road which had conveniently put it out early for the collection later that day. He made his way back to his lodgings, collected his belongings, tidied the room and left Mrs Browning a mauve and grey ten shilling note on the pillow and headed out the door. He needed to catch the train for Truro before the balloon went up.

Chapter Twenty Four

It was on the Saturday that the Major had left his parents' house early for the drive down into the extreme west of Cornwall. He followed the twists and turns of the A30 beyond Penzance and made his way to Chapel Carn Brea. Here amongst the Bronze Age cairns and barrows on the last hill in the country before America stood a new Chain Home Low radar station. The Major drove up the rough lane to the gate. The station consisted of a few nissen huts on the east side of the hill and the main radar building with its rotating antennae on the summit.

The Major was informed that its remote location, its place within the defences of the Land's End peninsula and the defended locations nearby were its main defence. Certainly its barbed wire fence was designed more to keep the moorland livestock at bay than any enemy incursion. Those working the radar felt air attack was their greatest threat especially as back in June the Land's End hotel was bombed with one fatality when the target was probably the RAF radar station at Mark's Castle nearby. The Major thought back to his own recent visit to Mark's Castle and his lunch at the hotel. How many of the casualties in this war were a case of wrong place wrong time. He looked out across the vista to Cape Cornwall and the waters beyond where the crew of HMS Registan had suffered on that fateful night in May. Peace would come with a huge price tag and he resolved never to forget that, but for now it still had to be won and he pressed on with his visit.

Heading back to the A30 the Major turned towards Land's End and was soon stopped at a roadblock manned by troops from the 7th Battalion of the Duke of Cornwall's Light Infantry. Here at Treave was the outer ring of the Restricted Area that protected the installations of the Land's End peninsula. A check of the papers, a look in the boot and the Major was soon allowed through. He drove past the anti-aircraft battery on Trevedra Common that he'd heard about in the Gun Control Room at Penhale House, and then as he passed the school at Sennen he turned down into Cove Road. He went a short distance until the road began to drop down the hill and pulled into a field on the right where a couple of huts stood. Here he had arranged to meet the young lieutenant commanding the troops in Sennen for a guided tour. It was a cordial meeting as the Major remembered the officer called Jarrett from his time at the Depot in Bodmin back before the war.

Pleasantries exchanged the tour began at a pillbox at the top of the hill. Jarrett led him down the steps into the rectangular pillbox. Inside it was brick built. Jarrett explained that the regiment here in the summer of 1940 had built it of brick. His men had tested it when they arrived with a Bren gun and were alarmed at the splinters that flew off, so decided an outer wall of Cornish granite was in order, so the pillbox had this double protection. They had covered it in soil and grass to disguise it from the air. The Major peered through the embrasures and commented that it wasn't well sited to cover the road up from the beach. He took Jarrett back outside and the two men climbed on the roof and the Major pressed his point.

“I suggest you simply add on an extension with a couple of embrasures that will do just that,” he said to the young officer whose face showed a little concern that the tour wasn’t getting off to the impressive start he’d hoped for. They moved down the hill to where a Type 24 pillbox stood with a panoramic view across the sweep of the bay. It had a small courtyard to the rear where a Lewis gun was mounted on a post for anti-aircraft protection. The Major complimented the two soldiers on duty for their explanation of their arcs of fire from the embrasures. Jarrett then pointed to another pillbox nestled in the hedge just below Maria’s Lane and explained that covered the road and the Cable House. The Telegraph Cable House stood out with its pristine white fence surrounding an immaculately cut lawn with what looked like a holiday chalet sat in the middle. There was a soldier on sentry duty outside the door. It was here that the trans-Atlantic cable came ashore bringing messages from Canada and the United States of America.

Jarrett then pointed northwards to a spot half way up the beach and explained that’s where the telephone cable came ashore and ran under the beach and up to a house in the small valley behind. He pointed out a couple more pillboxes in the distance covering the far end of the beach and then pointed to another further down the slope from where they were stood. It had a very unusual undulating roof running over its crescent shape.

“The roof is to make it look from the air like the granite boulders that are scattered across the hillside,” he explained. “There’s a second just a bit further over. Where the Vellan Dreath valley comes down to the bay the beach is mined and as you can see the coils of barbed wire stretch the length of the beach, although some of the storms play havoc with it. We've replaced sections of it twice during the time I've been here."

"I see there are two more pillboxes down where the road runs along by the beach towards the lifeboat station," said the Major. "Are there any others further on?"

"No, very quickly the cliffs rise and provide the natural protection against an invader. There's the coastguard look out at Pedn Men-du but no pillboxes," replied Jarrett. "The Home Guard patrol the cliffs while we defend the beach and the cables."

"So how many men do you have to repel any invasion," enquired the Major.

"We have eight hundred in the Land's End restricted area. Three hundred are based down at Porthcurno, I have one hundred and fifty here at Sennen and the rest are spread over the area manning the roadblocks, protecting the radar stations and wireless stations. There are eighty in the local Home Guard units and then there are the RAF and naval personnel at their various installations, the largest of which is RAF Sennen, the Chain Home radar station." The Major was impressed the young lieutenant was on top of his job and he told him so.

"Just improve the arc of fire on that top pillbox to make it harder for an enemy tank to make it to the top of Cove Hill and sort some camouflage for that cable hut and I think you have pretty much got things here covered," said the Major as his parting shot. He climbed back into his car and headed out the gate for the short drive to Porthcurno.

It was with a yawn that Elizabeth lifted the bonnet of the three ton army truck. It had been a late night last night but that didn't mean the checks on oil and water in the engine would get done by themselves. However, it had been a good evening and she had enjoyed the time with some of the ATS girls away from camp. There had been a variety concert down at the Public Rooms on Mount Folly with a group of ATS girls taking part and so Elizabeth and half a dozen others had gone down to watch.

The concert had started on a high standard with a performance by Stanley Coleman and the Bombshells doing a Hawaiian dance routine to music played on a guitar. The young Jamaican's tap dancing was superb. Next came a dance routine from young girls in Mrs Bassett's Concert Party followed by a tenor solo from one of the Depot soldiers. Elizabeth chuckled to herself as she removed the dipstick and wiped it with an oily cloth. The two soldiers who had done a comedy routine of wisecracks had made everyone laugh.

"Three old men are out walking," one of them had told the audience last night. "The first one says, 'Windy isn't it?' The second one says, 'No it's Thursday.' The third one says, 'So am I. Let's go get a beer!'" Another one stuck in Elizabeth's mind.

"The recruiting sergeant asks a new recruit, 'What is your date of birth?' 'July 3rd,' he replies. 'Which year?' 'Every year!'" The barrack room comedians were followed by four girls from the well known Bodmin Concert Party "The Queer 'uns." They performed a musical piece from one of their popular pantomimes.

The ATS girls had performed a song and dance routine that contained a number of old favourites such as 'Roll Out The Barrel', 'Little Brown Jug' and 'Bless 'Em All'. It had proved popular with the soldiers who made up the largest part of the audience.

The highlight of the evening had been the appearance of Major Mills as a dame. He sported a blue dress held in at the waist with a wide belt, a fur over his left shoulder, a hat with a veil and numerous rings of fake pearls around his neck. His rendition of 'Kiss Me Goodnight Sergeant Major' brought the house down. Elizabeth felt sorry for his daughter Miss Mills who had to follow her father. Dressed in a long floral petal pattern dress she sang several patriotic songs and then led the audience in 'Abide With Me' and 'God Save The King.' The evening had been to raise money for the Mobile Canteens Fund and had notched up £27 2s 6d. Elizabeth was still whistling to herself as she crossed the parade ground and headed inside for lunch.

Chapter Twenty Five

The Major enjoyed the drive from Sennen, turning left at Trevescan and following the winding lane until he came to Poljigga famed for its Land's End Vineries. He was astounded to see here next to the old smithy was a pillbox that had been disguised as a bus stop. The two soldiers on duty at the roadblock soon let him through and he passed the Methodist Chapel at Little Trethewey and then turned right by the milk factory and dropped down into the valley. He hadn't gone far before another roadblock stopped him at Bodellan. Here he was made to get out of the vehicle while his papers were checked. He had to open the rear doors and boot for the soldiers to thoroughly check his vehicle. The Major was impressed they were doing their job irrespective of the rank of the driver. He thought the West Yorkshire Regiment at Hayle could learn a thing or two from these DCLI lads. But that's how it should be as Porthcurno was designated a Vulnerable Point and had been classed Category A – to be defended at all costs.

The Major was allowed to proceed and drove down the hill to the telegraph cable station which was owned by Cable and Wireless. The deserted valley in west Cornwall had been chosen in 1870 as the place to bring the telegraph cables ashore from the Empire and it had grown into the most important communications hub in the world. The Major's visit here was to be in two parts, one with the Station Manager Mr Bell and the other with the duty Captain of the troops guarding the valley.

The Major was met by Mr Bell and shown into the office block that was painted in camouflage colours. Mr Bell outlined the brief history of the station and explained that fourteen cables currently came ashore to a small hut just above the beach. The station superintendant said that getting London to realise the strategic importance of the station had been a battle. When the Munich Crisis occurred they were given a police guard. When war broke out the policemen were armed with First World War rifles. In May last year the Chairman of Cable and Wireless had written to the government requesting help. The reply acknowledged that the station was of national importance but said defence plans for the area were secret so he couldn't be told. He could try forming a unit of Local Defence Volunteers! Needless to say a few heads were knocked together and within a month Porthcurno was told of plans to build a bomb proof shelter in the hillside adjacent to the current station. The job was given to the firm that had constructed the Mersey Tunnel, Edward Nuttall & Co., and using over two hundred Cornish miners from the St Just area they had commenced work on the 25th June.

"We now have a fully functioning cable station with its own generating facility and water supply built in two large tunnels in the hill. We opened at the end of May when the Chairman's wife, Lady Wilshaw, conducted the ceremony," concluded Mr Bell. "So let's go and have a look, shall we?"

The Major followed him outside to where a concrete portal housed an entrance into the tunnel. There was a soldier on sentry duty and papers had to be shown to get past. They came to a large blast door. It was a foot thick and had a circle of yellowy-green gas detecting paint in the centre. They stepped into a small ante-chamber and had to go through a second similar door. Then they were into the instrument room full of machines and contraptions that whirred, moved, punched tape with a score of people moving from one to the other checking that all was working as it should. There were two cross tunnels to the second parallel tunnel that contained the engine room, ventilation plant, battery room, wireless room and various offices for management and the engineers and a repair workshop. In the rear cross tunnel there was a door that led to the escape route. A flight of over one hundred steps led to the surface in case the entrance was bombed and became blocked, the staff inside the station could still get out. The two of them climbed their way up making two turns before coming to another set of two blast doors. The sentry let them through after checking their papers. Mr Bell laughed and said,

"Yes, even I have to have my papers checked. My wife Ruby has to have a pass to go down to the beach for a swim, and any staff that are not of British nationality are unable to request a beach pass."

They emerged back into daylight at the top of the valley from an entrance chamber whose roof was a yard thick to protect the entrance from aerial bombardment. There were two more soldiers on duty at a sandbagged position who duly saluted when they saw the Major. The Major acknowledged the salute and took in the view. In the field to the east was the camp for the soldiers with a couple of nissen huts and various wooden buildings. Off to the north was one of the large concrete water tanks that supplied the station with water. As he looked across the valley the Major could make out various troop positions, some just sandbagged into the hedgerows, others of more permanent construction. They descended once more into the tunnels and eventually arrived back at the entrance where the Major was to receive a surprise.

"Lieutenant Colonel Liddell, sir, how nice to see you," said the Major saluting and then putting forth his hand to shake that of the commanding officer of the 7th Battalion Duke of Cornwall's Light Infantry. "To what do I owe this pleasure?"

"Got word from Sennen that you were on the prowl, so I thought I'd pop down from Camborne to see you and take a look at A Company here," said the senior officer whose ribbons showed he was the holder of the Military Medal.

"Word travels fast," said the Major instinctively wondering if the sudden appearance of the regimental top brass was to head off some shortfall in the security arrangements he was about to be shown. The Major also greeted the two Captains present, one from the DCLI and the other from D Company of the 11th Battalion of the West Yorkshire Regiment. Fifteen of the Yorkshiremen had guarded Porthcurno through the winter months but since the prospect of invasion had risen its ugly head again troop numbers had multiplied. The Captains led the officers down the path towards the beach. When out of earshot from the Captains Liddell turned to the Major and said,

"Between you and me, I've got word that we are being reorganised in August and I shall be replaced. They are moving 7th Battalion's HQ to Falmouth and calling us the 30th. That way

Hitler thinks we have more battalions than we actually do!" The Major was incredulous.

"Yes, guy called Mulock coming in to replace me, so I thought I'd take the chance to get down west and have a good look at the dispositions. I'm off to D Company on the Lizard on Monday and B Company in Fowey after that," explained the Lieutenant Colonel. They soon arrived at a small hut with one shuttered window and a door. There was a sentry posted outside.

"This is what we are here to guard," said the DCLI Captain with a slight touch of sarcasm. "Fourteen cable ends in a small hut." Then seeing the unimpressed looks on the faces of the two superior officers continued,

"Sirs, may I point out our defensive positions to you. On the beach we have scaffolding across the width of the beach. Just behind that we have the flame fougasse which can be triggered from any one of three points. There is a control pillbox over there on the east side, another on the west just there." He was pointing to a small square pillbox with two large embrasures nestled just above the cliff. "It can also be triggered remotely from within the tunnels. The Petroleum Warfare Department have put two storage tanks one on either side of the valley." The Captain adjusted his footing and then continued.

"Just north of the control post is a crescent shaped pillbox, four embrasures to the beach, one to the rear. It has been built with a double wall so as to withstand substantial bombardment. The blast wall is nineteen inches thick. All the posts are connected by a trench system. There is a pillbox just there to cover the middle of the beach. Up on the cliffs either side we have a Type 24 pillbox, one at Respletha Cliff and the other at Percella Point. Both have rear courtyards for anti-aircraft guns. Further west on the lane down to the church is another pillbox, and east there are two pillboxes either side of the coastal path. The pillboxes were built by men of various Scots regiments when they were here last summer. Some of the men have left their names in the cement on the rock behind the one on Percella Point. Argyll and Sutherland Highlanders and the Black Watch, if I recall correctly," said the Captain looking at his Yorkshire counterpart for confirmation. He simply nodded. "At least they built decent positions, walls eighteen inches thick and good fields of fire covering the beach and any seaborne approach." The Major acknowledged the good work done.

"We then have sandbagged positions running along the top of the valley back to the pillboxes by the road into the valley. We also have a Z Battery positioned in the west side of the valley," the Captain continued.

"Ah yes," interrupted the Major. "Mr Bell was telling me about this. Apparently last November you had the battery but no ammunition. He said Cable and Wireless Chairman Mr Edward Wilshaw wrote to the Colonial Office demanding something be done about it."

"It was," said the Yorkshire Captain. "We got the ammunition in February." Lieutenant General Liddell raised his eyebrows.

"Desperate days," said the Major. "At least we are better prepared should Jerry decide to visit us this year. You've got the men you need to keep your perimeter secure and to respond to any landing?" The Major looked at the Captains for a response rather than the commanding officer.

"Yes, we have three hundred men based here in the valley and a further five hundred in the Land's End Defended Area," said the DCLI Captain.

"One of the best defended places in the country," said the Lieutenant Colonel unable to resist interjecting.

"Things have improved drastically since the winter," said the Yorkshire Captain. "We then had to work very closely with the Home Guard when there were just fifteen of us on duty at any one time."

"No problems?" asked the Major.

"Just one incident when an alert went out for downed airmen. A plane had crashed in flames over near St Just and it was thought the crew had escaped. A man was discovered in a farmyard behaving in a furtive manner. The Home Guard were called out and apprehended him and brought him to the guard room at the cable station. He was questioned in both English and German but no one could get any response out of him. Eventually they called the police who were delighted they had captured a British man who had escaped from police custody on his way to psychiatric hospital."

"Bless him. Any air raids?" enquired the Major.

"Just a couple. Rospletha Farm got hit but fortunately the Hoskings family weren't at home. Then on 6th May this year when they dropped 15 high explosive bombs which all fell in the fields around Roskestal Farm. There was one unexploded bomb that bomb disposal had to come and deal with."

"You have the explosives necessary if you had to retreat and blow the station?" asked the Major.

"There is no retreat from here, sir," said the DCLI Captain. "Our orders are to defend at all costs, down to the last man. There's no leaving the valley. I understand the cable station staff have plans for wrecking the cable connections once they have sent a final emergency message to the colonies. We do have the explosives to destroy the entrances but they would only be put in place at the last minute so as not to raise concern among the civilian staff over being trapped within the tunnels. No amount of explosives would collapse the tunnels. They are hewn out of solid granite. Fifteen thousand tons of it were brought out to make the underground station."

The Major decided not to appraise them of the Auxiliary Unit just a mile or two away with their hideout on Crean Hill whose main task was to deny the use of the cable station to the enemy. The small party began to make their way back up towards the Cable Station. Suddenly a whistle sounded from the top of the valley side. Its shrill cry was then echoed by a couple more as the two Captains looked at each other.

"What's that?" enquired the Major.

"That's the signal that there's an unidentified intruder within the perimeter. Usually it's just a farmworker who's taken a short cut but we stand to until they've been identified and passes checked," said the Yorkshire Captain.

“Permission to leave you and check it out, sir?” the DCLI Captain asked. It was the Lieutenant Colonel who replied.

“Permission granted. Go ahead.” The Major wondered as the Captain sprinted up the hill what drama might unfold for them today. A stray farmworker or an escaped patient perhaps.

Chapter Twenty Six

Sat in the Colonel's office at 76 Tirpitzufer, Berlin the Colonel had pulled out a large envelope of aerial reconnaissance photographs and thrust them into Johann's hand. He had looked at them and then turned them sideways unsure of just what he was supposed to be looking at. They seemed to show a small beach on the coast with a valley running up from the beach with various houses and buildings dotted about the valley. He had looked up at the Colonel for enlightenment.

"This is the Cable and Wireless telegraph cable station at Porthcurno in west Cornwall. It connects Britain to its Empire. It also used to connect England with a cable to Brest, but the British destroyed that soon after we conquered France," explained the Colonel. He went on. "The large rectangular building is the cable station and to the north and south of it there seems to be some earthworks. We want you to find out what it is the British are constructing. This is probably the most important task on your mission. Getting that information back to us is vital. If we are to invade we have to capture the cable station and cut off Britain's communications to her Empire. That's why the Fuhrer singled out Cornwall in Directive No 16 last summer, so I cannot stress how vital this information will be to our invasion plans." Johann had thought the Colonel had made himself abundantly clear.

Now crouched in the hedgerow gazing across the field to the rectangular building he had seen in the reconnaissance photograph, Johann pictured the scene in Berlin back in early

May and heard the Colonel's words ringing in his ears. The building was now painted in green and brown to camouflage it against the wooded hillside. To the north of the building Johann could make out two concrete portals, entrances, he presumed, to tunnels into the hillside but as to what purpose he could not tell. To the south was a large earthwork, possibly the spoil from digging out the tunnels. It had been planted with grass seed which was only beginning to turn the giant bank green. There was nothing for it. He would have to get a closer look.

He spotted a footpath that went diagonally up the valley side behind the cable station. He would head down into the valley, cross the road and try and see what he could see from the other side. He spotted a couple of nissen huts in a field on the far side. He would have to stay north of those, but with his haversack slung over one shoulder he could easily be mistaken for a farm labourer returning home across the fields.

He decided to follow the hedgerow down towards the valley as it provided the best cover to get closer. He got down to the corner of the field and stopped to peer over the hedge to consider his options for getting down to the road. As he looked into the large field to his right, he received quite a shock. About three hundred yards in front of him was a rocket battery. He recognised it as an anti-aircraft weapon and there were several soldiers clustered round it. That ruled any progress in that direction out, so he went over the hedge in front of him which brought him into a small field backing on to a house. He crossed the field and as the house was at a level lower than the field followed the hedge down to a gate which led him out onto the road.

Johann looked left and right. There was no sign of anyone. He crossed the road and followed the lane opposite which would take him towards the path he had spotted earlier. What Johann soon discovered to his horror was this roadway was actually the drive to the cable station. About ten yards ahead branching off to the left was the footpath he wanted. There was no sign of anyone so he decided to press ahead. Just as he was about to turn up the path a soldier walked across the driveway up by the cable station. He didn't look in Johann's direction at first but then seemed to sense some movement and turned and saw Johann. Johann kept walking and disappeared from sight. The soldier shouted something which Johann didn't catch but decided he wouldn't stay around to find out what had been said. He broke into a run. The hill was steep but Johann kept his pace. All of a sudden the shrill tone of a whistle pierced the air. What he didn't realise is the soldier had walked down the drive to where the path left it, looked up the path and couldn't see anyone so blew a whistle. Johann realised he had been spotted and an alarm was being raised. He decided to head through the shrubs on the hillside off to the left rather than keep to the path. It was a wise choice as another whistle soon came from further up the path. He pushed through the undergrowth and as he reached the top of the valley passed a large concrete tank which he correctly guessed was part of the water supply system for the cable station. He broke out into a patch of open ground where there was a wireless aerial set on a concrete plinth. He headed for the hedge in front of him, scrambled over it and found himself in a large field. Staying close to the right hand hedge he traversed the field, went through the gateway and into the next. He could hear several whistles coming from the direction of the valley behind him so just kept running.

The gateway out of the field took him alongside some farm buildings and he was looking for the track that would lead him to the road. He then decided that would not be wise in case the soldiers had a vehicle and came along the road looking for him. He then spotted a style in the hedge off to the right and decided to take that path. Fortunately the hill had plateaued and he soon found himself over the summit and heading downhill towards a small hamlet. As he got to the final field before the houses, he slowed to a walk so as not to arouse suspicion. He let himself through the gate and walked out into the middle of the little hamlet. He started down the road to his left, saw a sign for the Logan Rock Inn and thought about going in there, but decided it was the kind of place the British would look for him. So he retraced his steps and went down the road in the other direction. On his right he came to a small chapel. He opened the gate, walked the short distance to the front door, tried the handle but it was locked. He came back onto the roadway and as he passed the end of the chapel noticed there was a small outbuilding built onto the end of the chapel, partly hidden by that very English of kiosks, a red telephone box.. He guessed the outbuilding housed the toilet, so tried its door. It was open. He went in, locked the door and sat down. Here he would rest until it was dark and then he would make his way towards Penzance. He opened his haversack, took out an apple and began to eat it, his exertions having made him feel hungry.

The Major, the Lieutenant Colonel and the West Yorkshire Captain arrived back at the entrance to the cable station. Stood outside the guard room was the DCLI Captain holding a map in one hand, pointing with the other and issuing orders for his men to search certain areas. He paused as the others joined him.

"Young male seen coming up the drive and then sprinted up the path. Unidentified and as yet not apprehended," he said.

"Have you got a description of him?" asked the Major.

"Yes, the soldier who saw him described him as a young man in his twenties, blond hair, carrying a haversack over one shoulder," replied the Captain.

"Captain," said the Major with an urgency that startled the officer. "You have a major incident on your hands. That description fits a German agent currently on the loose in Cornwall. He has been active in west Cornwall, St Erth, St Ives, and we think he's been in Falmouth, so it is no surprise he has shown up at a location like this. You need to get all available men to secure the station and to do a sweep across the countryside above the valley. Do you have any vehicles at hand?"

"Yes, we have one armoured personnel carrier and one truck," said the Captain. The Major took his map and said,

"Then fill them with your men and get up the road. Keep a look out as you go but try and get ahead of him. Get to this road down to Pemberth Cove and then post sentries all along it. We can trap him between the main road and the sea."

"I've already sent word to the pillboxes by the coast path," said the Captain.

"Good, but we need a party to work their way along the coast path. When we've got enough men we will then do a sweep across the fields to the sentries on the Penberth Cove road and hopefully we'll flush him out in the box we have created," replied the Major. The Lieutenant Colonel spoke up.

"I can take a few men in my car and we can drive to the farms off the main road, see if there have been any further sightings and alert them to be on the lookout." The Captain detailed two men to go with the Lieutenant Colonel and his chauffeur. Men were beginning to appear from every direction as the general alert had obviously gone out. Some went straight to their duty stations; others came to the guard room for orders. The Major was impressed that within ten minutes the Captain must have used or had at the ready about one hundred men and more were arriving all the time.

The first farm the Lieutenant Colonel stopped at was Trethewey. He found the farmer's wife. She had seen nothing but said she would report it immediately if she saw anyone she didn't recognise. She said no one was likely to come round the farm buildings as they had some of the soldiers billeted in a nissen hut by the cowshed.

The next farm was Trendrennen. Here they found a farm labourer who had seen a man pass along the footpath to Treen less than half an hour ago. Encouraged by the sighting the Lieutenant Colonel pressed on and took the lane into Treen. He stopped at the inn and the two soldiers went to investigate. The door was locked but their banging brought the landlord who was about to lecture them on opening hours until he heard they were searching for a suspicious person. The landlord had seen no one. They drove up the road, past the empty phone box to the dead end by the chapel. The two soldiers were dispatched to search the chapel. The front door was locked, so they peered in through the two side windows but there was no sight of anyone inside. They tried the toilet shed door but found that locked too.

"All locked up," was the report as they got back in the car. "Do we need to find the caretaker or the minister?"

"No," said the Lieutenant Colonel. "If a fugitive was going to hide in a building like that, there'd be some sign of forced entry." He drove on down the hill to the junction to Penberth Cove. Here the truck was parked and every hundred yards on the road down to the sea was a soldier standing sentry. At the end of the lane they found the armoured personnel carrier and a small cluster of soldiers who were watching the coast path and the small bridge over the stream. The Lieutenant Colonel reported that there was a sighting of a man heading eastwards so encouraged them to keep a good lookout. He then decided it was time to report back to Porthcurno. He had done his bit. The foot slogging would be left up to the infantry.

On his return to the cable station he found the Major and DCLI Captain discussing what else they could do, such as alerting all the road blocks heading out of the Land's End Defended Area. The West Yorkshire Captain had gone up the hill to organise the sweep of men across the fields towards the Penberth valley now that they had sufficient manpower to make it effective. The Lieutenant Colonel reported the possible sighting by the farm labourer and asked if there was any more he needed to do. When the Captain said they were now sitting and waiting to see whether they could flush out the fugitive, he suggested he might take his leave and travel back to Headquarters. He did say that if more men were needed he could make some available, but as it seemed they were only dealing with one man the Captain probably had enough with the three hundred at his disposal.

It was three hours later a rather despondent West Yorkshire Captain reported that his men had combed all the fields and paths from Porthcurno to Penberth Cove and back and found no sign of their wanted man. The coastguard above Penberth Cove had seen nothing. On their return sweep they had checked all the sheds and outbuildings at Treen, causing quite a stir amongst the inhabitants, and again at Trendrennen Farm. It would start getting dark in an hour.

The officers decided all they could do was to post guards along the main road and the lane down to Penberth Cove and on the coast path to keep an eye on the perimeter of the search box they had created. Sentries would be doubled at all the usual posts in the valley and at the cable station. It would be a long night of watching and waiting.

The Major made a series of phone calls to London, to Major Hare in Bodmin and to Bob Dunstan in Falmouth to alert the various powers that be to the fact that he suspected that the agent had broken cover. The last one was to his parents to inform them he would not be home that night as something had come up that needed his attention. The DCLI Captain then provided a most welcome cup of tea and a sandwich as the three officers settled down for the duration.

Chapter Twenty Seven

It was dark when Johann slid back the small bolt on the toilet door and gingerly peered round it. There was no sound or sight of anyone. He opened it a bit wider and could see down the lane. It was clear as far as the corner. He moved to the corner of the chapel and peered round. It was clear up the lane as far as the farm gate. He then opened the door of the telephone box and went inside. Rummaging in his pocket for the right money, he picked up the receiver, pushed in his two penny coins, and pressed button A. Very quickly the operator responded and asked what number he wanted. He gave the number he had been given in the park in Falmouth and waited to be connected. After what seemed like an eternity, the operator's voice said,

"Putting you through now, sir," and he then heard the distinctive tones of the lady from the park. Johann gave the codeword, a time and then gave a map reference. As soon as he'd said it, the line went dead. She'd hung up. He pressed button B but no change was proffered so he replaced the receiver and stepped outside.

He headed for the farm gate, climbed over it so as not to risk it making any noise if it was opened, and stepped into the field. He walked alongside the hedge in an easterly direction. He had decided he would walk through the fields rather than on the paths and roads as this increased the danger of being spotted and picked up. He walked at a steady pace, using gateways where possible, or scrambling over the Cornish hedges where necessary. He was soon heading down into the valley that runs down to the picturesque Penberth Cove. As the valley side steepened small trees covered the slope and he was able to move from one to the other until he came to the road. He glanced left and right, but saw nothing of concern, and stepped down onto the road. He had emerged just below Chmoy corn mill at a spot where the stream came close to the road and so with a run and a leap he jumped the stream and landed in the undergrowth on the far side. He steadied himself, paused and listened and when he heard nothing other than the running water, turned and pushed his way through the undergrowth and began to climb the far side of the valley. At the top he merged back into farmland and continued his trek across the fields.

He made good progress until he reached the valley running down to Lamorna Cove. Having crossed the road, he found the stream too wide to jump and so had to settle for wading through. He hoped his shoes and the bottoms of his trousers would dry by daylight so as not to attract attention to himself. The eastern sky was just beginning to lighten as he arrived in a field overlooking the small fishing port of Mousehole. He had not seen anyone on the whole of his journey. Only once in a farmyard some way off had a dog barked. He made his way out onto the narrow coastal lane and followed it down into the village. Being Sunday morning all was quiet. Most curtains were still drawn as he tramped through the narrow streets and came out overlooking the harbour. His eyes were scanning for a suitable vessel to take.

He spotted one that he thought he would be able to manage over against the north pier. He made his way round the harbour and onto the north pier. He went down the steps and scrambled aboard the little fishing boat with a small cabin to give some protection to the wheel. He looked at the controls, turned behind him, lifted the engine cover, found the crank handle and decided he would be able to start it. He then decided he would untie her before starting the engine to minimise the amount of noise before he was heading for the harbour entrance and his getaway out past St Clement's Isle. He climbed back up the harbour steps and was untying the boat when a cry came from a man who had emerged onto South Cliff by the Ship Inn. He gestured frantically and continued to shout. Johann knew he wouldn't have time to start the engine and make his get away so there was nothing else to be done but to turn and flee on foot. The man was now running round the harbour towards Johann so Johann sprinted off the pier and up the first street leading away from it. From Quay Street he turned into Commercial Road, cut across Southview Terrace and slowed to a walk as he turned up the lane up the hill. There was no sign of anyone following him or raising any kind of alarm.

What Johann couldn't see was that the man who had spotted him was the owner of the vessel he was trying to steal and had gone round onto North Pier to check on his boat and make sure it was properly secure. Only when he had done that did the man head to the Police House in Porthenys Place to wake the constable and report the attempted theft of his fishing boat. Johann passed the village school and continued up the hill at a steady pace. There was no sound of any vehicle heading his way in pursuit so he decided to keep on the lane until he heard something approaching. He soon found himself in the village of Paul renowned for being the resting place of the last natural Cornish speaker Dolly Pentreath who died in 1778 and one of the places in Cornwall ravaged by the cholera epidemic of 1833. Now that his plan for escape had fallen at the first attempt Johann decided it would be better to travel out of the area that was being searched for him and to make his escape further east. He walked down the hill into Newlyn and headed for the railway station in Penzance.

There were a few people around in the town as he made his way into the station but no one took any notice of him. He had to wait for the ticket office to open so took the opportunity of buying a bar of chocolate from a Reeves vending machine on the platform. When the booking clerk opened the hatch Johann wandered over and bought a single ticket to St Austell on the 8.50 train, the first departure of the morning. Just fifteen minutes before departure the coaches were propelled into the platform by a Castle class locomotive that was going to the haul the train to North Road in Plymouth. Johann boarded and collapsed into a seat exhausted after his overnight jaunt across the Cornish countryside.

It was nine o'clock Sunday morning when the telephone in the guardroom rang and the caller asked for the Major. It was the police to report the attempted theft of a fishing boat in Mousehole and the suggestion it could be linked to the wanted man. It was with a sigh the Major replaced the handset and turned the two bleary eyed Captains and said,

"You can stand your men down. It seems he'd escaped the cordon and tried to steal a small fishing boat in Mousehole early this morning. Unfortunately he ran off before he could be apprehended. The police have sent a couple of men down to the railway station and the bus station in Penzance to see if he tries to use public transport to further his getaway, but I think we've lost him for the time being."

"So where was he when we swept the area between here the Penberth valley? Twice!" The West Yorkshire Captain sounded frustrated and indignant that he and his men had been outsmarted by this individual.

"I've no idea," replied the weary Major. "But I shall use your toilet before I take my leave and go and get some sleep." When he returned he said to the two Captains, "Remain vigilant. He may try and return if he didn't get a look at what he came for. I'd keep your double sentries for another forty eight hours. If I get any news I'll let you know. If you have anything else suspicious I want to know right away." With that the Major found his car and started on the long drive back to his parents' house and a welcome rest.

Chapter Twenty Eight

Mrs Trevennel didn't bring her usual wake-up cup of tea and let her son sleep in on Monday morning. He had refused to go to bed when he'd arrived home the day before; instead insisting on making a series of phone calls. Just what he had been caught up with she and her husband were never to find out. Anyway it had been a relaxed afternoon and now after tea the three of them were sat in the drawing room. Mr Trevennel was sat reading the Monday evening Packet which had just arrived via the paper boy on his bicycle. Quite why her husband insisted on having the paper delivered that evening and not with the daily one the following morning she could never understand. Still, who was she to begrudge him his little luxury now that he had retired and was unable to pick it up on his way home from the office?

"What despicable men!" Mr Trevennel suddenly blurted out.

"Who's that, dear?" his wife enquired.

"Apparently five men were in court this morning for stealing off a bombed ship. Five pleaded guilty and another was charged with being an accessory."

"That's awful," said Mrs Trevennel. "What did they take?"

"Food, milk, coats, oilskins, shoes, boots, handkerchiefs, jerseys, socks, soap, packets of soap flakes, binoculars, and a piano accordion," replied Mr Trevennel as he scoured the report for the details.

"Here let me read you what the Mayor, Mr Gill, the chairman of the magistrates, said," he continued. "'The Bench are unable to regard these cases as simple pilfering. We must have regard to the circumstances. If the police do not know, some of the magistrates do know that at the time this so called pilfering took place there were the bodies of men lying on the ship. Those men sacrificed their lives for their country and before their bodies had been removed these defendants had taken their effects. The excuse that there was no guard on board only aggravates the offence. It appears to the Bench to be nothing more or less than robbing the dead.'" The Major knew this had to be referring to the Registan.

"What sentence was given?" he asked.

"The five were fined twenty pounds which had to be paid today or they would face imprisonment for two months with hard labour. The accessory was fined two pounds," Mr Trevennel said from behind the paper. His mother asked the question the Major wanted to know.

"What did the accessory do?"

"Two of the accused asked him – apparently he was a deckhand on a tug - to dispose of the piano accordion. He threw it overboard," came the response.

"Perhaps a month's wages will help them to appreciate the valiant effort our sailors are making to keep us fed and supplied," said the Major. His parents voiced their agreement with their son's sentiment and the conversation moved on.

It was the following morning that a long distance phone call came for the Major. When he got to the phone it was the office back in London.

"Can't say anything on this line, Trevennel, as it's not secure, but you may just want to get yourself over to St Erth and their intelligence officer will update you."

Mrs Trevennel couldn't understand the need for her son to dash out without waiting for lunch but she was wise enough to know one didn't ask questions. She stood at the window and listened to the car roar away up the drive.

When the Major arrived at St Erth he pulled up into the field and parked his car next to the mess hut. Mr Reardon greeted him and showed him to his office where the station intelligence officer, Holmes, was installed. Mr Reardon held the door open and lingered hoping for an invite to join them which wasn't forthcoming. Somewhat put out that his office had been hijacked, he closed the door and went and found something to do.

"Well done for getting here so quickly, sir. It's been an interesting morning. I'll come straight to the point. We've had some messages from Station X that have led to some direction finding detective work, if I may call it that. Lots of this is new to me but I'll relay what I've been told to tell you. Don't know if you know, but our chaps captured a German submarine back on the 9th May. A boarding party from HMS Bulldog brought out various code books and an intact Enigma machine." The Major's eyes opened wide at the significance of the scoop. Holmes continued. "X have been able to break the

Reservehandverfahren. I'm told this is a cipher used by the German navy when no Enigma is available." The Major nodded. He'd had a few conversations with Jack Plumb who headed up the team working on the naval cipher when the Major had visited Station X.

"Thus we have been able to make sense of a greater number of messages which I'm told is beginning to prove useful. The reason we've called you in today is that we've decoded a series of messages calling for the pick up of someone. The signal strength is such that it has to have been transmitted from this side of the Channel." That really caught the Major's attention but he said nothing. The intelligence officer continued, "St Erth have been involved in trying to get a fix on the signal. At the moment all we can say is that it's somewhere along the coast between Falmouth and Fowey. London are sending down one of their mobile units to go into the area to pinpoint the transmission site. The mobile should be here and operational by tonight."

"Good work, Holmes," said the Major understanding now why London wouldn't reveal anything over the public telephone network. He glanced at the door wondering if Reardon was lurking outside. "How much does Reardon know?" he asked.

"He's aware we are onto an illegal transmission in the UK from the direction finding work the St Erth DF station has been tasked to do, but he knows nothing of what I've just told you," Holmes replied.

"He must wonder why his humble station intelligence officer suddenly takes over his office," said the Major.

"He'll have to keep wondering. I'm not authorised to reveal my true position in intelligence," said Holmes. "He'll have to keep thinking I'm a humble station intelligence officer who won't let him in on so much. I'll think of some sop to feed him," said Holmes with a smile.

"That's about it. As soon as we get a confirmed location on this transmission requesting a pick up we'll let you know. Or if any of the messages give an actual pick up point, though I suspect these things are often agreed in advance so may not be mentioned. The DF work is our best bet."

"Thanks very much. It seems after his failed attempt to steal a boat for the journey home he's broken wireless silence and appealed for help." said the Major standing up. "Keep up the good work. We'll get this one yet."

Mr Reardon stood at the door to the wireless hut watching as the Major drove off the station. He sensed the Major had met Holmes before he introduced them today but what was going on in the murky world of military intelligence was beyond him. He crossed to the mess hut and decided to make Holmes a cup of tea.

Chapter Twenty Nine

Elizabeth was looking forward to seeing the Major again. As soon as she realised she would be free on Thursday evening she had phoned through to Bosvarren to see if there was any chance of him being in the Bodmin area. The Major had switched a couple of his unannounced visits around so would spend the day working in and around Looe and would then be able to spend the evening in Bodmin with Elizabeth before heading home to his parents' house for the night. Having finished her duties at four she had plenty of time to get herself ready. The Major was due to pick her up at six and they had reserved a table at the Royal Hotel for dinner at half past. The big decision was should she step out in uniform or should she wear an evening dress for the occasion. She got both ready as she couldn't make a final decision.

The Major's day had progressed well. He had seen pillboxes, anti-tank walls and dragon's teeth at Talland Bay before venturing into West Looe for a visit to 392 Battery of 557 Coastal Regiment. The coastal gun battery had been established in July 1940 right in front of the Nailzee Hotel and the gun emplacements housed two four inch naval guns. Nearby was the command post and a little behind on the hill the battery engine room whilst down at the water's edge was the searchlight battery which had just become operational in March. The sloping cliff was covered in a tangle of barbed wire coils and there pillboxes either side, one towards Hannafore Point and the other overlooking the Blind at the entrance to the harbour. He was shown around by Captain Burch who said he was used to the routine having had an inspection by Lieutenant General Franklin, the Commander of 8 Corps, back in March. The Major was satisfied all was done that could be done.

He then met up with Major Horace Ross, a stern looking man with a dark moustache, commanding officer of the Home Guard who showed him the two three pounder guns the Home Guard manned to defend the harbour boom and the pillboxes to defend East Looe beach. His visit finished with a tour of the boatyard owned by Mr Frank Curtis as they were building the wooden hulls for Motor Torpedo Boats. The Major saw a deck being laid and then a couple of motor launches alongside the quay where additional fitting was done. Frank Curtis also explained he had a similar operation at Par Docks where the wooden hulls were then towed round to Charlestown Harbour where under the huge covering roof the navy fitted their engines.

The Major was satisfied with a day well spent as he cut down into the Glynn Valley for the road into Bodmin. He negotiated the roadblock at Glynn Bridge which brought back memories of the first day Elizabeth had driven for him and then headed up the hill to Carminnow Cross taking the lane that cut down to the side of the barracks. As he pulled up by the gate to the Keep out stepped Elizabeth, looking as radiant as ever. She had been chatting to the guard as she waited and she turned and gave him a cheeky wave as she got in the front passenger seat because he wouldn't believe that it was a Major who was her date. The sentry was left open-mouthed as the Humber Snipe pulled away and headed down St Nicholas Street.

The Major parked the car outside the front entrance of the hotel in Fore Street. As he went round and opened the door for Elizabeth he winked at two boys stood on the pavement opposite admiring the car. They disappeared into the hotel and headed for the bar. They had just taken their first sips when the hotel manager came in looking rather flustered and said that he had a message for the Major. He took him away into his office and told him he should telephone the number he had scribbled down for the Major. A man had called about ten minutes ago and said it was urgent he speak to the Major.

Elizabeth, glass in hand, had followed him out into the reception and stood wondering what had come so urgently for the Major and whether it would spoil their evening. She was surprised to see Beryl, one of the ATS girls, come in on the arm of a dashing young sergeant from the Royal Army Ordnance Corps. The young couple were told by reception that all their tables were booked and the earliest they would be able to dine was eight thirty that evening. Beryl looked crestfallen as her plans for the evening were obviously evaporating.

The Major emerged from the office in a hurry and was pleased to find Elizabeth in the reception area.

"We need to go straight away," he said with a look on his face that indicated there was no discussion to be had on the issue. Elizabeth leaned and whispered something in his ear. The Major turned and said to the bemused receptionist,

"This couple will take my reserved table. We won't be needing it ourselves." He then took Elizabeth by the hand and led her out of the hotel as the delighted sergeant and Beryl called their thanks to the disappearing figures. Once in the car the Major spoke with a seriousness in his voice.

“I can take you back to barracks or you can come with me, although I cannot guarantee that we’ll have a meal this evening.”

“I’ll come with you even without food. At least we’ll spend some time together. But can you tell me what this is all about?” she said not quite knowing what she was letting herself in for.

“The agent that we’ve been trying to apprehend has been located in Gorran Haven,” said the Major as the car pulled away sharply up the street causing the two young lads to stop and look back in amazement. “We believe he has been trying to signal to the enemy for a pick up and our wireless detection boys have pinpointed the transmission to Gorran Haven.”

“At least we can drive there,” said Elizabeth with memories of the steep climb down to Lantic Bay the last time she’d had a romantic evening with the Major interrupted. “So you are going to arrest him? Are the police coming?”

“We haven’t yet located the person, just the wireless signal. But we need to be there in case his pick up is for this evening. The person I spoke to is going to alert the police commander and the Home Guard. He was also going to try and contact the coastal gun battery at Pentewan and get some regular troops from there. So there will be plenty of back up.”

“Won’t all that lot descending on the place scare him off for tonight?” asked Elizabeth.

“No, the police and Home Guard are going to throw a cordon around the village blocking off the roads that lead away from it, but they won’t go into the village until they get the order from me,” replied the Major. After clearing the roadblocks at the edge of Bodmin the Major put his foot down as he headed down the A30 until he could take the St Austell road just beyond Lanivet.

“I don’t believe it,” said Elizabeth after a pause as she let the Major concentrate on his driving. “The last time I put this dress on for an evening out in Bodmin I was whisked away to go chasing the enemy. I put it on this evening so I would look lovely for you and what do you do to me? Whisk me away to go chasing the enemy again. Only this time I’ve not even had the chance to enjoy dinner!”

“I’m sorry,” said the Major glancing sideward to see whether Elizabeth’s complaint was serious. The grin on her face came as a relief. He liked the way she teased him, though he realised that neither of them would get dinner for quite a while. He tried to redeem himself.

“You do look absolutely ravishing,” he said with another glance at the beautiful young woman sat next to him. He thought that she looked more beautiful, if such a thing were possible, every time he saw her. Elizabeth turned and gave him an appreciative, loving smile.

The Major made good progress through Bugle, Stenalees, Carthew and down into St Austell before meeting another roadblock on the Pentewan road. They were quickly let through and they headed down the wooded valley towards the coast. They fell silent as their thoughts turned to all the various scenarios they might face ahead. At Pentewan they had another Home Guard roadblock to contend with before climbing the hill to take the Gorran road. Here they passed long sections of wall that had been built as a job creation scheme for veterans who had returned from the Great War and struggled to find work during the Great Depression in the Twenties and Thirties. Several Cornish landowners had worked together to devise and run the scheme that saw broken down Cornish hedgerows replaced with concrete block and cement walls that provided employment for destitute men and food on the table for their families.

The Major drove through the hamlet of Gorran Churchtown and as he came to the turning for Gorran was stopped by a Home Guard soldier. As he got out of the car he could see there were several others by the roadside. One of the men, Dunn, came and spoke with him.

“Corporal says to tell you he’s sent a messenger on a bike over to Hemmick to Mr Bunney of the Gorran Home Guard to guard the coast road west from Gorran. They were told to block the junction from Vault above Penare. Corporal is setting up a roadblock at Trewollock and he says he phoned the Mevagissey police house but got no answer so the constable can’t be home.”

“Good work,” said the Major. “Have any of the Home Guard down in Gorran Haven been alerted yet?”

“No, our instructions were not to tell them so as not to alert the wanted man. Mr Bunney’s been told not to tell them either,” replied Dunn. “We are going to move round the corner to Cross Close so we have all exits from the village covered.”

“Just don’t let anyone into the village yet without my authorisation,” said the Major. “She’s with me. She’s an ATS Corporal,” added the Major seeing Dunn look at the front seat passenger in the car and wonder if the instruction started with the pretty beau in an evening dress. The Major got back in the driving seat and eased the car off round the bend. He drove slowly down the hill, round several bends before taking a narrow lane off to the right just past Rice Farm. At the top of the hill he passed another farm before turning left into a drive way that took him to a large house with a commanding view of the beach that stretched away towards Dodman Point. The Major pulled up in front of the house and said,

“Strange, I don’t see the van.” He got out and indicated Elizabeth should follow.

“Who were you expecting to meet?” she asked. At which point someone came round the end of the house. The Major turned and said,

“Holmes. There you are. I couldn’t see the van.”

“Trevennel. Good to see you. I heard the car come up the drive. And this is?” he asked looking at Elizabeth wanting to know her security status before answering the Major’s query.

“Corporal Treluckey,” the Major said doing the introductions. “She’s part of my staff. You can talk freely. Her evening got interrupted by your call hence the garb.” Elizabeth shook the man’s hand wondering if the Major had just recruited her into his mysterious world of military intelligence. She also thought she would have to educate the Major into the niceties of evening dresses so he wouldn't refer to it as 'garb'.

"We've got the van in a field behind the house," said Holmes. "We are at the top of the hill behind a belt of trees so we can stay out of sight of the village. From here we have been able to pinpoint the signal to the hill the other side but can't say which of the properties it is coming from."

"Let's have a look," said the Major and the three of them trudged across the edge of the field by the tree line to where the Morris van was parked. Holmes opened the rear door and inside was an operative in headphones sat at an array of knobs and dials. Holmes introduced everyone and then gave the Major a more technical breakdown of what they had achieved thus far. When he was finished the Major asked,

"Can we get a view of the properties in question from up here?"

"Yes, a little further on a path goes down through the trees. You can see them from there without breaking cover," said Holmes shutting the van door. The party made their way to where Holmes had indicated and stayed amongst the trees to look across the harbour and Little Perhaver beach at the houses in question.

"So what have we got here?" asked the Major looking for some interpretation to the view that greeted them beyond the trees.

“From the beach going left to right we have Ben Vista, that’s the one right down by the edge of the cliff,” said Holmes.

“Got it,” replied the Major.

“The next slightly larger property is Blue Point. According to Mr Fischer Williams here at the house, that’s the home of Captain Richardson and his wife, so possibly not that one.”

“You know who Mr Fischer William’s daughter has just married, don’t you?” asked the Major. Holmes shook his head. “Hart of ‘Five’, the guy who found Ter Braak dead in an air raid shelter in Cambridge back in April. Hart believed he’d shot himself because he’d run out of food.”

“Oh really,” said Holmes somewhat surprised. “Small world. I always remember Hart as the chap who was sent to investigate the spy messages on the telegraph poles left for enemy parachutists. After travelling miles across southern England in response to the reports he declared that they were the serial numbers put on each pole by the GPO. So he’s the son-in-law of the couple here. Now I know why you suggested we came to this location, Trevennel.”

“There’s usually a madness to my method,” grinned the Major. Elizabeth laughed. She was beginning to experience that.

“Next is Caprera and the one behind is Pabyer,” said Holmes continuing his guide to the properties. “Moving right we’ve then got Red Rock, Longships and the last one is Perhaver named after the beach. So we are pretty certain it’s one of those from where the transmissions are being made.

Usually about nine o'clock based on the couple of days we've been here."

"Does anyone in the village know you are here?" asked the Major.

"Only the couple at the house and I've made them sign the Official Secrets Act. The position of the van is such that it is out of sight from the coast path that is used by the Home Guard and the Coastguard. We are hidden by the trees from the properties on the other side of the valley."

"Good, good," said the Major. "So how do we determine which house is sending the transmissions without scaring our man off?"

"We were looking for you to have the answer to that one," said Holmes.

"I suppose I could go and have a walk around in the village," said the Major thinking out loud.

"Not dressed in that uniform," said Holmes. "As soon as you are spotted swanning around word will get round the village something's up and our man and his helpers will soon get to hear and they'll shut up shop and our efforts have been wasted."

"He can't, but I can!" It was Elizabeth whose intervention caused the two men to turn and look at her.

"I knew there was a reason why you put that dress on this evening," said the Major with a wink in his eye. It was agreed Elizabeth would head down into the village on a scouting mission and as they walked back towards the Major's car the two men were trying to give her suggestions of what her line should be if anyone asked what she was up to.

"I'll take the car," announced Elizabeth. "It will then appear I've just arrived in the village. It also gives me a speedy means of escape should I run into Johann." The Major was a little taken back at her boldness but agreed to her request.

Elizabeth eased the car up the drive and down Lamledra Hill before turning right onto the Canton. She drove until she could see the beach and then pulled in on the right by an old lime kiln and parked next to the Western National Omnibus noticeboard displaying its timetable. She got out of the car and looked around deciding on a course of action. She looked round the corner and viewed the tiny cottages lining the very narrow Church Street.

The Major and Holmes had returned to the vantage point in the belt of woodland. The Major knew at the first sign of trouble he would sprint across the field and down into the village leaving Holmes to return to the van to summon help. He looked at his watch. It would start going dark in an hour.

Elizabeth walked up Church Street a short way and found a narrow cobbled alleyway leading off to the left. It went by the quaint name of Rattle Street. Praying for inspiration as she went, Elizabeth decided to knock on the door of the second cottage along. She rapped her knuckle on the door and waited. A woman in her fifties answered the door and looked a bit taken aback at Elizabeth in her fine dress. Elizabeth spoke first.

"I am so sorry for troubling you but I am looking for my boyfriend. I believe he's come to stay in Gorran Haven but I've got completely lost and am wondering if you could help me."

"What's the address you be looking for?" said the woman still a little suspicious of this pretty young lady.

"That's just the problem, you see, I don't have one. He simply told me to take a left and said I'd then see the house on the left but I don't know where I am now," said Elizabeth trying to sound convincing as she made up the directions.

"Well this is Rattle Street. This place is called Chyandour, so it ain't here that you is looking for," said the woman.

"He's Dutch, my boyfriend. So do you know of anyone in the village who's got a Dutchman staying with them?" asked Elizabeth with a sudden flash of inspiration.

"Hang on a minute," said the woman finally feeling sorry for Elizabeth. She turned and shouted into the depths of the cottage. "Tim. Timmy! Do 'e know of anyone who's got a Dutchman come to stay?"

"Who's asking?" said a deep Cornish voice from the shadows behind the lady of the house and soon the large muscular frame of a fisherman emerged beside his wife. He eyed Elizabeth up and down and then spoke to his wife.

"Mrs Dymock said the other day that Olive Greenbaum had told her that her nephew had come to stay unexpectantly. But I don't knows whether he be Dutch. I did see him last couple of nights. He's been sat on bollard at end of harbour with a fishing rod looking out to sea but I ain't seen him catch anything," said the fisherman with a critical tone that implied the man in question didn't really know what he was doing.

"So where does Mrs Greenbaum live?" asked Elizabeth sensing there wouldn't have been too many strangers come to stay in the village in the last couple of days.

"Well if you go up Church Street here to the top and then turn right. Keep going up that lane, way past where you see the Coastguard houses off to the left, and keep going. When it starts going flat it's the only house on the left." Elizabeth thanked the fisherman's wife and walked back down the cobbles to Church Street. When she saw the steepness of the hill she thought about going back for the car but decided she didn't fancy negotiating it up the narrow hill and decided that an on foot recce was the order of the day.

She passed the Anglican Church, passed Mount Zion Chapel tucked away behind a cottage and then came to the top, so following her instructions turned right. Within a few moments as she rounded the bend the houses along the cliff top came into view. She saw the one she wanted behind two impressive properties and thought about going up the lane for a closer view but decided against it. She didn't want to be responsible for alerting anyone to anything so turned around and headed back down the hill to the car and drove back to find the Major.

Chapter Thirty

There was a buzz of excitement amongst the Home Guard men as the Major outlined his plan of action. A couple of the Gorran Home Guard who lived at St Goran had joined them as they were on their way to do a duty along the cliff path to Vault Beach during the night. The men at Cross Close would head down into the village, half to go down the main road knocking at the homes of a few of the Gorran Home Guard to join them, half to go along Cook's Level and then to meet again at the junction of Chute Lane and Church Street. Those at Trewollock would take the footpath that emerged into Cliff Road and approach the house from the other direction. They would also put two men in the field behind the house to make sure no one escaped from the rear. The Major looked at his watch.

"It is now twenty past nine. We'll move in on the house for ten o'clock. By then it will be completely dark and will shield our approach. Those of you with watches synchronise them with mine." As the men adjusted the time where necessary, a police car drew up with two policemen from St Austell. They explained they had been sent by Major Hare. The Major recapped the plan for their benefit and assigned one to the Cross Close group and one to go with the Trewollock group.

Those joining the Trewollock Group were dispatched to go and join them and explain what they had to do. The Cross Close group then moved in line down the hill with the Major and Elizabeth leading. Progress was good and by ten to ten the Major had twenty men around him at the top of Church Lane. He hoped the other group were in place ready for the kill. At five to ten he gave the order to advance. They passed Rose Cottages and the driveway down to Schovella and ducked down below the hedge as they progressed up the hill. By one minute to ten they were at the wooden gate. It had a small brass plaque on it saying ‘Pabyer.’ Out of the shadows emerged four Home Guard and a policeman who had come from the footpath.

The Major silently opened the gate and walked up the path. The Home Guard fanned out in the garden with rifles trained on the front door. The Major indicated that some should go round to the rear of the property and called the two policemen forward to join him. They looked a little nervous wondering whether the armed force aimed at the door was an indication of the response expected from behind it. The Major walked up to the front door and knocked loudly.

After what seemed like an age he could hear movement and the sound of the black out curtain being pulled back. Two bolts were slid back and finally the door was opened just enough for a head to appear.

“Mr Greenbaum?” asked the Major.

“Yes,” came the rather nervous reply as the householder caught sight of the two policemen.

“Can we come inside and talk to you?” asked the Major politely. At this the man reacted and tried to slam the door but the Major’s army boot was already wedged in the gap and the Major leaned into the door with his shoulder and forced it open. He immediately pulled his pistol from it holder and ordered the startled Mr Greenbaum to put his hands up. The two policemen then burst into life and rushed inside as the Home Guard in the front garden sprinted towards the door. The policemen burst into the lounge to catch sight of Mrs Greenbaum throwing a bundle of papers on the fire. One of the officers grabbed her hand and pulled her away while the other stooped to retrieve what he could from the flames with the coal tongs. Three Home Guard with fixed bayonets burst into the room and Mrs Greenbaum's legs buckled beneath her and she sank into an armchair with the policeman still holding her by the wrist. The Home Guard pointed their rifles at her and the policeman decided he could let go.

In the hallway the Major had got two of the Home Guard to take Mr Greenbaum into a different room so he couldn't communicate with his wife and to cover him with their rifles. He then ordered a search of the rest of the house to see if there were any other occupants. Whilst there was evidence of the spare bedroom having been used recently, they found no one. Eventually the Major made his way back into the lounge.

"Where is he?" he asked Mrs Greenbaum as he holstered his pistol.

"My husband. I don't know. What have you done with him?" she replied, her eyes showing a belligerence that provided little comfort to the Major.

"Your supposed nephew, you know, the Dutchman," said the Major.

"You're too late," she said with a hint of satisfaction in her voice.

"Where's he gone?"

"I don't know. He left earlier this evening." The Major persisted in his questioning but could get nothing further from her. He tried to extract information from the husband but he was less co-operative than his wife. The Major's spirits fell. 'Don't say this blasted Abwehr agent has got away from my clutches for a second time.' His thoughts were interrupted by a young Home Guard who had just come into the lounge. His Corporal spoke.

"What is it, Rowse?" he asked.

"I have found some wireless equipment in an upstairs room, Corporal, and I thought the Major might be interested."

"Good work Dennis," said the Corporal as the Major went to follow the young soldier upstairs. It was a room which was built into the roof with a window that overlooked the harbour and the beach. The walls appeared panelled and were painted white. In one of the panels near the window Rowse went and pushed against the panel near the vertical stile. There was a click and the panel swung open. Inside sat on a couple of shelves was a SE-88/5 short wave five Watt wireless transmitter and receiver, a product of the German Abwehr manufactured in 1938.

"How did you find the cupboard?" asked the Major.

"I was checking the panelling for any empty spaces behind where a man could be hiding. When I got to this one it sounded hollow so I kept tapping away and eventually found the spot to press to open it," said the young Home Guard with a sense of pride.

"You've done very well," congratulated the Major. "Don't touch it. The police will need to dust it for fingerprints and it will be used in evidence against the traitors." The Major returned downstairs and said to the policemen,

"You can arrest this couple under the Treachery Act." The policeman stood up, adjusted his helmet and pronounced to Mrs Greenbaum,

"I am arresting you for conduct designed or likely to give assistance to the naval, military or air operations of the enemy." He went on to read Mrs Greenbaum her rights and then produced a pair of handcuffs for the sullen faced woman. His colleague then went into the dining room to do the same to Mr Greenbaum. The Major turned to the Home Guard Corporal and said,

"We need half a dozen men to stand guard here until the police can transport the couple from the property. The police may want you to guard the property until they can get the Security Service and their detectives to comb it for evidence. Otherwise you can stand your men down. The excitement is over for this evening." The Corporal acknowledged the order and the Major stepped outside for some fresh air to clear his mind.

He saw Elizabeth for the first time since he'd entered the garden of Pabyer and went to speak with her. She simply put a hand on his shoulder knowing he would be feeling the pain of not getting the quarry. The Corporal detailed six Gorran men to guard the property and asked four of the Mevagissey men to assist the police in guarding the prisoners until the police removed them. He then dismissed the rest and told them to return to their normal duties.

Half a dozen set off for the cliff path on the opposite hill and young Len Billing decided to head down the path to Little Perhaver Beach. Part way along, just below Schovella on the cliff edge was a lookout built by John Ball for watching the coast during the long nights of duty. Billing went to find his father in the lookout as he was a coastguard and was on duty with Ball. Keen to tell them of the excitement in the village he walked along the path and stepped into the lookout with its long embrasure making it easy to scan the horizon between Turbot Point and Pen-a-maen Point. He was part way through his tale when John Ball told him to be quiet. He obeyed but was puzzled as to why.

"There," said John Ball. "I heard it again. Engine of a boat." All three men now strained their ears and, sure enough, the throbbing of Daimler Benz marine engines could be heard. The two coast watchers grabbed their binoculars and scanned the darkness looking for any sign of the vessel that sounded as if it was approaching.

"It's going at some speed," said Charles Billing.

"E-boat," said John Ball. "There!" he exclaimed. "Just east of the Gwineas." Charles adjusted his binoculars to pick up the dark silhouette of the wooden hull speeding across the water.

There was little stern wake which made it difficult to spot but both men now had their binoculars trained on the vessel.

"Go back and get your men down to the harbour," said the senior Billing to the junior. Len didn't need telling twice. He was out of the lookout and up the path like a shot. He ran up to Pabyer where the Major and several of the Home Guard in the front garden had stopped their conversations as they'd also heard the engines. Billing shouted from the gate,

"E-boat. Incoming!"

The Major suddenly realised that the pick up was happening now. There was still a chance to apprehend the fugitive. He turned to the Corporal.

"Six men stay here. The rest, half to the harbour, half to the cliff top to give covering fire." He then took off down the lane at breakneck speed. He was glad it was downhill all the way. He knew their best chance was to get to the agent before the E-boat made the harbour because with its armament of 20mm cannon the Home Guard wouldn't stand a chance with their rifles.

As he passed the anti-tank barrier by the entrance to the beach he could see the E-boat approaching at speed. The tide was high but he thought there was enough sand for him to be able to make it across the beach and onto the harbour wall. As he stepped onto the sand the E-boat did a sharp turn sending a wave of white water cascading towards the beach. Its captain then throttled back its engine so it slowed as it came alongside the end of the pier. For the first time the Major saw Johann. He had been crouched in the shadows on the wall but he now broke into a run timing his sprint so with a great leap he landed on the deck of the E-boat where a couple of sailors scrambled to catch hold of him as the Captain gave the engine room the order to throttle up and speed away into the night. The Major fired his pistol in the direction of the boat, more in anger than in any hope of hitting his man. The gunshot brought a volley of rifle fire from the clifftop. The anti-aircraft gun on the stern of the boat then opened fire causing the Major to dive onto the sand as a 37mm shell smashed into the wall behind him. The boat headed out beyond the Gwineas and was gone.

EPILOGUE

The following morning at Bodmin Crown Court there was an in camera sitting in Courtroom No 1 where Mr and Mrs Greenbaum were committed for trial at the Old Bailey. The hearing lasted ten minutes but it gave the Major some satisfaction that at least some good had come out of last night's events in Gorran Haven. Johann's contact in Cornwall had been apprehended and would face the full force of British justice. He wondered if there were others. He was still sore about Johann getting away again but he looked forward to taking Elizabeth out for the dinner she had missed the previous evening. The Greenbaums were transported by MI5 to London to await trial and to see whether under interrogation they would reveal anything more about their treachery in Cornwall.

Elizabeth was in uniform when the Major picked her up at the end of her day's duties. The Major didn't comment. With her hair tied up under her cap she still looked gorgeous and the Major was delighted when she linked her arm into his as they stepped into the Royal Hotel. It was busy as usual, a mix of service personnel and locals but everyone was busy going about their business totally unaware of the events that had unfolded on the Cornish coast the night before. No word would appear in the Cornish Guardian or the Western Morning News until the end of August when a small paragraph would report that two foreign nationals resident in Britain were executed at Pentonville prison under the Treachery Act. Tonight, however, the Major's thoughts were entirely on Elizabeth. They dined well and then decided to take a walk after the meal. They headed out of the town along Copshorn Road where apart from one man out taking his dog for a late evening walk they didn't see a soul. At the top of the hill they stopped and looked back at the view across to the Beacon. The Major gently pulled Elizabeth close to him and kissed her on the lips. She responded to his display of affection and the kiss was lingering and passionate. When their lips finally parted, the Major caught Elizabeth's gaze and said to her,

"I love you." Her heart jumped for joy and her eyes smiled.

"I love you too," she said and they kissed again. The sky had turned a bright red as they walked back down the hill past the jail. The sun was setting in the west giving promise of a better day tomorrow.

Johann sat on the plane flying him to Berlin lost in his own thoughts and ignoring the other military passengers around him. He had arrived safely back in Cherbourg on the Schnellboot just after two o'clock in the morning. He had wondered what had happened at the Greenbaum's house as there seemed to be gunfire from the clifftop as the boat left Gorran Haven but a burst from the stern gun had silenced that. He ran over in his mind all that he had to report to his superiors back at Abwehr headquarters. Details of his activities at Falmouth, details of the harbour defences including the new guns and searchlights, details of the pillboxes on the beaches along the coast, details of the new rations in England, and examples of the everyday paperwork which future agents would have to grapple with if they were to avoid detection. He had confirmed that the wireless station at St Erth was not of major importance as it was only guarded by the Home Guard. The only thing he had been unable to ascertain was the purpose of the tunnels recently built at the cable station at Porthcurno. The fact that he had been able to penetrate the defences and get so close should impress his superiors and hopefully shield him from any criticism of being unable to supply the exact information they had requested.

He smiled to himself as he thought how he had managed to evade capture by holing up in a lavatory. He was glad too he had managed to get away successfully on the Schnellboot. He was sure it was the figure of the Major who had appeared on the beach just as his rescuers arrived. He told himself that one day he would have the pleasure of finishing off his nemesis. For now he was looking forward to the good food of Berlin and then some well deserved leave back in the Harz mountains with his grandparents. Where would the Abwehr send him next? He hoped it wouldn't be east. He didn't speak Russian. Maybe they would send him to spy on the British in North Africa. Somewhere warm would be nice, he thought. He'd prefer that to promotion and an office job, or simply training others. He was looking forward to his next mission already. But the delights of his grandmother's Schnitzel would have to come first.

HISTORICAL NOTE

While I have made every attempt to make the background to this story as accurate as possible, any interpretation or representation of historical figures or events, whether national or local, is purely mine based on the available sources. The main characters and their actions are the creation of my imagination as this is a work of fiction. For example, while I am not aware of any wartime inspections of Hayle Power Station, it is well documented that the SOE agents who crippled the Pessac Transformer Station using limpet mines had practised on Luton Power Station getting in and out unnoticed with a subsequent inspection by Cecil Clarke revealing to the subaltern in charge of the guard a number of the limpet mines (which Clarke had developed using his children's aniseed balls) attached to vital equipment. The ruse I have used for getting the men into the plant was used in more modern times by the SAS when they were inspecting one of our nuclear power stations.

Sabotage at Falmouth Dockyard was a reality, although I have taken events from over four years and squeezed them into a short period of time.

The work of the Radio Security Service at St Erth was a well-kept secret. As radar was to the public the big secret of the war, I have had elderly villagers still insist to me that it was a radar station and that has even found its way into some Historical Environment Record entries. The wireless intercept station was guarded by the Home Guard during the invasion scares of 1940 and 1941 but that was withdrawn later in the war. Don Wallis, who served there in 1943, recalled catching the specially provided bus from his billet in Penzance and it driving up the lane to drop them at the gate with no security to go through at all. However, I am sure the siting of a POW Camp at St Erth later in the war was to reduce the risk of bombing.

The HMS Registan plot of the war graves section of Falmouth Cemetery is one of the most poignant and moving places in the whole of Cornwall. When first shown it as a child by my father we wondered what the story was behind the white headstones. He knew there had been a fire onboard but could tell me little more. Much research and communications with some relatives of both those who survived and those who perished later, I was keen to tell the story of the last victim of the Bismarck. To include it within a work of fiction was simply borne out of a desire to get the story out to as wide an audience as possible. It was a joy to be able to reveal to one family that the relative they thought had shown cowardly behaviour by being one of the officers who survived in the lifeboat was in fact one of the heroes of the night by his brave and selfless actions that saved the lives of many. It has been heart breaking to tell others that the sources currently available give no indication of just how their loved one died. It is to thousands of sailors in both the Royal Navy and the Merchant Navy that Britain owes its survival in those dark days of 1941 when it stood alone against the might of Nazi Germany. Their service and sacrifice led to the subsequent victory in both the Battle of the Atlantic and ultimately the war.

A number of the wartime locations referenced in the novel still survive but many are on private land and should only be viewed with permission. Some are on publicly accessible land

and can be viewed at leisure. The Admiralty Experimental Station at Perranporth is now the Youth Hostel so you could always go and stay! Many pillboxes and gun batteries, especially on the coast, have fallen to the ravages of coastal erosion and personal safety should always be a priority when visiting wartime locations as steep drops, sheer cliffs and mineshafts abound.

Again I trust the novel has made you get out the map, do some searching of your own, either on the internet or on foot, as you realise the enormity of the vital role Cornwall played in the war. The by-product of my research has been turned into some video-book style presentations which you will find on YouTube on the 'Phil in Cornwall' channel. They are entirely amateur, the camera work is definitely not professional, but they were a means of getting the history out there to a wider audience before it is lost as the wartime generation rapidly disappears from amongst us and the wartime infrastructure is destroyed by man or nature.

THINGS TO DO

(subject to government restrictions & guidelines)

For more on Cornwall in World War Two check out the YouTube channel 'Phil in Cornwall'. Here you will find numerous video-book style presentations of places and events in Cornwall during the war, with some documenting the remains that are still standing today.

Some places you may like to consider visiting:
The Porthcurno Telegraph Museum with its wartime tunnels;
Pendennis Castle, Falmouth;
Cornwall's Regimental Museum at Bodmin;
The RAF Davidstow Moor Memorial Museum at Davidstow;
The Cornwall at War Museum at Davidstow;
Trebah Gardens with its D-Day Embarkation Hard on the Helford River;
St Eval Parish Church with its memorials to those who flew from RAF St Eval.

The numerous small museums dotted around the county in places like Padstow, Bodmin, Fowey, Wadebridge, Liskeard, Launceston, Helston, Constantine, St Agnes, Liskeard, Lostwithiel, Looe, Mevagissey, Newquay, Perranzubuloe in Perranporth, Redruth, Saltash, Penryn and St Ives as well as the Royal Cornwall Museum in Truro and the Heritage Centres at Grampound, Gerrans, Bude, Callington, and Hayle are all well worth a visit. There is one near you so there's no excuse!

Look out for temporary exhibitions by the many local history societies across Cornwall that often appear just for a weekend but can give some insight into wartime events and life. Look out for my own Cornwall in World War Two photographic exhibitions that I use to help promote the books.

Check out the website of the Cornwall Railway Society. It is a goldmine of information and photos on Cornwall's railways. You'll also find my diary showing what happened on the railways in Cornwall during World War Two. The line described in this book is still running and well worth the ride for the fabulous views. There is a new Park & Ride facility at St Erth making it an easy way to visit St Ives.

And finally while you may still have members of your family who were alive during the war record their memories and tales – you will never regret it. Grasp their stories before it's too late.

A Map for Pat
Padstow
Launceston
Wadebridge
Bodmin
Newquay
Lostwithiel
Perranporth
Looe
Fowey
Portreath
Truro
Gorran Haven
St Ives
Hayle
Porthcurnick
St Erth
Falmouth
Constantine
Land's End
Porthcurno

BY THE SAME AUTHOR

ISBN 978 1 9998463 0 5

The first book of the trilogy that introduces the Major, Elizabeth and Johann in the invasion summer of 1940.

"Brilliantly written" "Gripping story" "Beautifully written"

Available at eBay, Amazon or from your local bookshop

COMING SOON

The third book of the trilogy will feature the build-up of American forces in the county prior to D-Day in 1944 when racial tensions from the States were played out in a number of Cornish towns.

It will reveal more of Major Trevennel's inner turmoil over his family as well as tracing the ups and downs of his relationship with Elizabeth.

Will the Major finally get his man?

Keep your eyes and ears peeled for news of its publication date.

CORONAVIRUS AND THE OFFICIAL BOOK LAUNCH

This book was due to be officially launched at the Gorran Haven VE75 Celebrations to be held at Haven Church in early May 2020. The coronavirus and the restrictions rightly put in place have seen that event postponed to an as yet unknown date. I decided to press ahead with the release of the book as many of you have waited over two years already and to help provide some new reading material to those in isolation and a welcome escape to all of us from the constant barrage of doom and gloom.

My thanks go to all at Haven Church for their help and encouragement and I look forward to the VE Exhibition and Thanksgiving Service with you when circumstances permit. Look out for details on the Gorran Haven village website or Haven Church website and why not come and join us at the event when Cornwall is open for business again.

A 2020 THANK YOU

to all who are working in the NHS, the Care Sector and key industries and services to support us all in our national hour of need. Many commentators have drawn parallels to our wartime struggle, be it in the increase in state intervention or Her Majesty Queen Elizabeth II citing Vera Lynn's "We'll Meet Again." Many from that wartime generation have been an inspiration to the nation such as Captain Tom Moore of the Duke of Wellington's Regiment whose one hundred laps of his garden raised so much money for NHS charities.

To the many unsung heroes across our nation, I add my voice in gratitude and admiration and pray we will be worthy of the sacrifice and that we will emerge a better nation out of this shared experience.

To all those coping with life in shielding, isolation, and lockdown, I dedicate this book. Enjoy the read!

May God bless you and keep you and give you His peace.

COPIES OF

NO SMALL STIR

ISBN 978 1 9998463 0 5

AND

A PLACE AND A NAME

ISBN 978 1 9998463 1 2

are available on Amazon or eBay
or from your local bookshop.

"Even unto them will I give in mine house and within my walls a place and a name better than of sons and of daughters: I will give them an everlasting name, that shall not be cut off."

Isaiah 56 v5.